THE
SEA DOG

BY

ARTHUR C. BARTLETT

ILLUSTRATED

CUPPLES & LEON COMPANY
PUBLISHERS   NEW YORK

CONTENTS

The Sea Dog

CHAPTER I

PIEFACE

THE clang of hammer against nail blended with the staccato yelping and barking of dogs at the famous Bersey kennels. And the more the hammers clanged, the more the dogs yelped and barked, for the hammers were sounding the knell of imprisonment. The dogs were being crated.

The little French island of Miquelon, just off the coast of Newfoundland, where the kennels were situated, was beginning to brighten up after the long, cold winter and the sloppy spring. The gentle sun of early summer was shedding its grateful warmth over the island, by way of reward for those who had borne the bleak blasts of a northern winter. Where a few months before had been huge drifts of snow, now was green grass—grass so green and rich that it seemed to invite all dogs in the neighborhood to come and romp and play,

9

to flex their unused muscles and to release themselves from the restraint which winter quarters had placed upon them.

But the dogs, instead of gaining the freedom of the bright, beckoning fields, were being confined in even smaller quarters than before. They were being crated. So they barked and yelped in natural disappointment as the relentless hammers sealed them up, away from the pleasant pastures for which their canine hearts yearned. And they yelped and barked at each succeeding lath, as it was nailed into place, cast another long shadow across the joyous sunshine.

Up in the lodge, on the little hill overlooking the kennels, John Bersey lay on his bed, his shoulders propped up with pillows so that he could look from his window at the proceedings below. John Bersey could neither bark nor yelp, and probably would not have done so if he could, but his eyes were as sad as those of the saddest dog in the crates below, and his heart was ten times as sad as his eyes.

John Bersey was as securely penned up as were the dogs. To be sure, no nailed

grates barred his way to the summer freedom outside, but the bars of illness
stronger than any sticks of wood, held him
in his bed. But though John Bersey,
throughout the fifty-odd years of his life,
had been one of those happily-constituted
persons who find their greatest pleasure
under the open sky, it was the most minor
cause for his sadncss now that he was unable to indulge himself in that pleasure.

John Bersey knew that he was dying.
But that, too, he could havc borne philo-
sophically under other circumstances. Life,
until recently, had been good to him, and
though he was by no means an old man,
he was not the man to grumble and protest
against fate now that it was about to with-
draw him from the good things it had
showered upon him.

The thing that made John Bersey sad
was the same thing which made the dogs
bark and yelp—that steadily clang of hammer against nail. To the dogs it meant
imprisonment. To John Bersey it meant
the end of all things. He knew what the
dogs could not know—that the crating was
no mere process of imprisonment, but a

preparation for shipping and sale, for the abandonment of the Bersey kennels, for the writing of the word "failure" after the name of the dying John Bersey.

For thirty years the name of John Bersey had meant anything but failure in the world of business. For twenty years it had meant anything but failure in the world of dog fanciers. But the tide of business had turned on him, and wiped out his success. He had come back to the lodge on the little island of Miquelon to die among his dogs, but now even the dogs would have to go. The very lodge itself, which had been the most humble, if the favorite, of his homes, had been sold, and he was only remaining in it because he was too ill to be taken elsewhere—and, indeed, had no other place left to go.

His only son, Wilson, was even now on the way to Miquelon from Europe, where he had been travelling, and John Bersey wondered how he would tell him that the Bersey fortune had vanished. He hardly knew this son of his, who had been brought up in expensive private schools or under the guidance of private tutors ever since the

death of his mother, when he was a little
lad. He hardly knew him, and yet it was
for him that he had worked, for him that
he had built up his fortune, for him that he
had tried to build it up still more—only
to lose all. For a little while each summer
father and son had used to live in the lodge
on the island, but of late years, as the boy
had grown older, even these brief sojourns
together had been given up, as Wilson
found little to amuse him on the island.
The father had continued to come, giving
to the dogs, whom he loved, the personal
interest that the son no longer seemed to
need. If he wondered, now and then, how
it happened that his son did not share his
interest in dogs, he quickly told himself
that the boy was young and busy with the
business of youth; that the loneliness of
advancing years would come soon enough,
and that then the son could turn to the
dogs and find them, as he had, a constant
spring of friendship and happiness.

So John Bersey had built his happiness,
planning for the happiness of his son, and
now all his plans were wrecked, and he
wondered how he could face the boy when

he arrived. The clang of hammer against nail. The barking and yelping of his dogs —no, not *his* dogs any more. John Bersey closed his eyes, and lay back in the pillows, passing a pale and emaciated hand over his closed eyes as though to wipe out the pain of what they had seen.

The door opened and a man and a dog entered the room. The leathery face that showed in spots under the man's whiskers marked him as one who lived mostly outside the protecting walls of houses. This was Joe Kirkup. He had been a fisherman years ago, but had retired from the sea to become the caretaker of the Bersey kennels. Just now he was also acting as nurse.

John Bersey laboriously turned on his pillow as he heard the door open. "Any news from Wilson, Joe?" he asked.

"No news yet, John," (In New York there were bank presidents who had never ventured to address John Bersey by his first name in their frequent dealings with him, but Joe Kirkup never thought of addressing him otherwise. He would not have given up the sea to become a menial for a New York financier. His status had always been that of friend, congenial spirit, and first lieutenant of John Bersey, the dog fancier.)

"I hope he comes—soon," said John Bersey.

This observation seemed to need no reply, and Joe made none, but busied himself with pouring some medicine from a bottle on the table into a glass. He handed it to the sick man, who drank it mechanically. He lay back quietly for a minute, then opened his pale lips.

"Joe," he said.

"Yes, John?" The rough, bewhiskered old man's voice was as gentle as a mother's.

"What are you going to do now, Joe?"

Joe knew that he meant: "What are you going to do after I die and the kennels are abandoned?"

"Me?" he said. "Why, I aim to get in some fishing by'm'by." Then he hastened to add, "Not so long as you need me, though."

"I know that, Joe."

The men fell silent, words seeming futile. Outside the hammering had stopped, and only the occasional wailing of the crated

dogs could be heard over the subdued singing of the surf, a half mile away.

At length John Bersey spoke again as
Joe sat rocking in a chair by one of the
windows. "The dogs, Joe, are they—all
ready—to go?"

Joe nodded. "All ready," he repeated.
"All but Pieface, here."

The dog that had followed him into the
room, having been lying motionless in a
corner, now lifted his head, and then rose
leisurely to his feet. He was a bull terrier,
a white dog of medium size with a short,
smooth coat; long, tapering muzzle; short,
erect ears; broad, flat skull, and a straight
tail which wagged endlessly.

"Good old Pieface," said John Bersey.
"Come over here."

Pieface came, tail a-wag, and placed a
pair of moderately dirty feet on the counterpane. He poised his ears to catch his
master's slightest command, and tried to
stretch his neck turtle-fashion in order to
get his friendly muzzle nearer the face of
the sick man.

"Good old Pieface," John Bersey re-

peated, grasping the dog's muzzle affectionately. "You can come up."

Pieface responded with alacrity, and
brought the other pair of moderately dirty
feet up on the counterpane. With his
tongue he lapped John Bersey's hand in
token of love, and then, at a word of command, settled down on the bed, keeping
his eyes eagerly on his master's face.

"You don't amount to shucks, Pieface,"
said John Bersey. It was a stock greeting,
and Pieface wagged his tail with extra enthusiasm in appreciation of what he understood to be a compliment.

As a matter of fact, the estimate was
more or less correct. As a show dog, Pieface was a total loss. He had been a
gangling, scraggly pup, and he was still far
from impressive in appearance now that he
had reached doghood's estate. The first
time John Bersey had ever seen him he had
burst out laughing at the half-serious, half-
comic face of the pup, and he had then and
there christened him Pieface.

But the very thing that had made him
laugh had also touched a deeper chord in
his heart, and John Bersey had come to

take a greater interest in the unimpressive
pup than in any of his various prize winners and prospective prize winners. "He's
such a lovable little clown," had been his
explanation to Joe Kirkup, and Joe, being
somewhat inclined to sentimentality himself,
had heartily agreed. Thus Pieface had become the reigning favorite of the kennels.

He had taken the privileges that went
with this high estate quite as a matter of
fact. When John Bersey was at the lodge,
there would Pieface be also, although no
other dog was allowed within those hal-
lowed precincts. When John Bersey walked
over the island, Pieface walked with him.
And when John Bersey left the island for
another of his long absences, Pieface gave
his companionship to Joe Kirkup, who
sometimes found it necessary, in his capac-
ity as trainer, to be severe with the other
dogs, but who found Pieface's every act
quite satisfactory. "You brazen hound,"
he might say, when Pieface had taken some
new and unprecedented liberty; but Pieface, understanding only the tone of his
voice, would take the words as admiring
commendation, which, in fact, they were.

It had been disappointing to Pieface to have John Bersey come back to the island and remain in bed in the lodge all the time, as he was doing now. He had tried several times to inveigle his master out for a walk and a romp, but without success. So he had been forced to take his exercise by following Joe around, just as if the master were not there. He had been very much puzzled, too, by the activities in the kennels, but he had known that he would be exempt from the crating to which all the other dogs were being submitted. Nothing like that could happen to Pieface.

And, fortunately, his conceit was justified—for the very reason of his comparatively small value. The man who had bought John Bersey's dogs had looked Pieface over and readily agreed to let his offer for the lot stand with Pieface excluded from the sale.

Now the other dogs were all securely crated up, and in a few hours they would be on their way to the mainland, while Pieface lolled comfortably on John Bersey's bed and heard John Bersey say, affectionately, "You don't amount to shucks, Pie-face."

Joe Kirkup almost said, "Lucky he don't too," but realizing that this reminder of his employer's financial straits might sound unkind, he left it unsaid.

Then John Bersey expressed the very same thought himself, though he addressed it to the dog. "And I thank heaven you don't amount to shucks, Pieface," he said, "for if you did, you would be going the way of your playmates."

Pieface lapped the emaciated hand, and cocked his head wisely. He liked to be taken into the confidence of this man-god of his, even though he did not know what it was all about.

Another period of silence followed, as John Bersey lightly stroked the dog's head. Then: "Joe," he said.

"Yes, John?"

"I had intended to leave you enough to make you comfortable for the rest of your life, Joe."

"Oh, well," said Joe, "I don't need any-thing. Don't be thinking about such things."

"I can't help thinking about it, Joe. And there's Wilson to think about, too."

"He ought to be getting here soon," said Joe.

"Yes, I hope so—and yet, it is going to be hard to tell him."

"You know, Joe," he resumed after a pause, "I have nothing left—absolutely nothing—except Pieface."

The dog, listening intently, bestirred himself slightly at the mention of his name. John Bersey scratched his neck, and he blinked happily.

"And Pieface," John Bersey continued, "is really as much your dog as he is mine."

Joe smiled faintly, thinking of the dog, but said nothing.

"If you want to keep him, you may," said John Bersey; "yet—Wilson—." He stopped, uncertainly.

"Of course you want Wilson to have him," said Joe.

The sick man sighed, and the dog looked up at him with inquiring eyes. Joe looked meditatively at the floor.

"Well, Joe, I would like Wilson to have him, in a way. It's not only that I have

nothing else to give him, because as far as
that goes he will be just as penniless with
Pieface on his hands as without him—a
little more so, in fact, for it will mean feed-
ing two mouths instead of one. It's not
that so much. But it's going to be a great
shock to the boy to find out that he has
nothing. It's going to be hard for him to
get along. He has never had any reason
to expect anything like this. He'll need
a real friend as he never needed one before,
and as I hope he'll never need one again, to
keep him from losing his bearings entirely
—a friend to cling to and pour his heart
out to. And you and I know that a man's
dog is his best friend. That's why I want
Wilson to have Pieface. You see?"

He lay quietly back in his pillows, exhausted by the long speech. Pieface rose
to his feet and stood as though protecting
his master from some unseen foe. Joe Kirkup nodded solemnly.

"Yes, John," was the answer.

Joe rose from his chair and walked to
the side of the bed. He took his employer's
pale hand in his horny one for a moment.
Then he motioned to Pieface to come down,

and the dog sprang to the floor. With the touch of a professional nurse, Joe adjusted the bedclothing.

"You'd better get some sleep now, John," he said. "Wilson ought to be getting here soon."

"Thank you, Joe,—for everything." John Bersey closed his eyes, and again his emaciated hand passed over them in a gesture of pained helplessness.

Pieface followed Joe Kirkup through the door, and Joe closed it lightly behind them.

CHAPTER II

WILSON Bersey was dressing for dinner in his hotel room at Brussels when the cablegram came. Cecil Wembridge, his Oxford tutor, who was travelling with him at John Bersey's expense during the summer vacation, took the envelope at the door, and laid it on the table while Wilson endeavored to get his necktie adjusted to suit him.

Wilson, having finished with the necktie, slipped on his coat and vest, smoothed them down, and surveyed himself complacently in the mirror. What he saw in the mirror was a youth of sixteen years, ruggedly built, perfectly groomed, and apparently entirely satisfied with himself. He then picked up the envelope, tore it open, and proceeded to read the message.

"I am very ill," he read. "Please come to Miquelon at once. Pay Wembridge." It was signed, "John Bersey."

Wilson's mouth gathered into a pout, and with a gesture of digust he tossed the cablegram down on the bed, where Wembridge was sitting. "Will you read that?" he exclaimed. " 'Please come to Miquelon at once.' Of all the places in the world, I have to go to Miquelon just when I'm starting to get a little pleasure out of life. I won't go, that's all. I won't go." He strode to the window and looked out, belligerently.

"But your father says he is ill," said Wembridge.

"Well, what of it?" stormed Wilson. Then, surprised at the bitterness of his own words, he added, "Oh, well, of course if he's really sick I'll go, I suppose, but I'll bet it's just an excuse to get me back to that hole. He goes down there and fiddles away his time with a bunch of yelping dogs, and he thinks I ought to make as big a fool of myself over them as he does."

"I'll find out what steamer you can get," said Wembridge.

"Oh, never mind now. There'll be plenty of time to-morrow. I'm not going to tear my head off rushing back there. I guess he isn't as sick as all that. Come on to dinner now."

"But, Wilson," remonstrated the tutor, "you don't know how ill your father may be. I think you had better do as he says."

"I don't care what you think," shouted the youth. "I'll go when I get good and ready, and not before. Who are you to tell me what you think? You're getting paid for being a tutor, aren't you, not a preacher? And that's another thing,—" he picked up the cablegram again,—" 'Pay Wembridge." Why doesn't he send me some money then? He must think I'm living on corned beef and cabbage and travelling on a bicycle. After I pay you I'm going to have barely enough money to get to Miquelon with. Of all the low-down tricks—." He threw the cablegram down again, and stood still, fuming.

"It's fortunate you don't care what I think," said Wembridge, "for if I should tell you what I think of you just at this moment, it would not be particularly complimentary. Shall we have dinner now?"

Wilson plunged his hands into his pockets, and followed Wembridge to the dining

room, where they ate in silence. After
the dinner, Wembridge, without consulting
Wilson further, looked up the steamers and
made arrangements for departure on the
next day, booking passage for the boy on
a steamer leaving Southampton on the day
following. When he returned to his room
later in the evening, Wembridge informed
him of the arrangements.

"Oh, all right," said Wilson; "there's no
fun travelling with an old maid like you
anyway."

They left next day, in accordance with
Wembridge's plans, and on the day after
that Wilson sailed, having grudgingly paid
the tutor the amount due him, and without
so much as a handshake of farewell.

All the way across the Atlantic Wilson
sulked. Accustomed to doing exactly as he
pleased, he felt deeply injured by being
forced to give up his plans for a summer
of travel on the Continent. He thought it
unreasonable of his father to be taken sick
at all, and particularly just at this time;
and if he had to be taken sick, Wilson
could not see why he could not be sick by
himself, instead of sending for him to come

home. In short, Wilson Bersey was much more interested in himself and in his own idle pleasure than in anything else in the world. Therefore he sulked.

Arriving at New York, he decided that their home there would be closed since his father was at Miquelon, so he established himself in a hotel. After taking account of his financial condition, however, he decided to go to his father's office and get "old Sanders" to advance him enough money to enable him to remain in New York a few days before exiling himself to Miquelon. Wilson's idea of remaining in New York a few days involved the expenditure of considerable money.

Accordingly he summoned a taxicab and was driven to the Bersey Building in the financial district. "Old Sanders," who had been his father's secretary as long as Wilson could remember, recognized him at once, but Wilson had never known the old man to greet him with such a peculiar manner,—half embarrassed, half pitying.

"I'm on my way down to Miquelon," Wilson explained, shaking the old man's hand in a rather patronizing manner.

"Oh, yes," said Sanders. "Yes, indeed. Of course."

"I'm nearly strapped," Wilson went on.

Sanders coughed behind his hand, flush-ing, and looked at the youth with that queer expression of embarrassment and pity. It made Wilson uncomfortable, but he told himself that "old Sanders" was merely get-ting "dotty."

"I wish you would let me have a little money, Sanders," he said. "Just a thous-and or so."

Sanders coughed again, and opened his mouth to speak, but seemed unable to say anything.

"I'll fix it up with Father when I see him," Wilson assured him.

"You haven't heard from your father, then?" asked Sanders, at last.

"Just a cablegram saying he was ill," Then Wilson, for the first time, bethought himself to inquire about the seriousness of his father's illness. "It's nothing serious, is it?"

"I couldn't say, really. I've heard that he was quite ill, but I don't know."

"Well, I hope not," said Wilson, dismissing the subject. "But if you will just let me have a little money now, I'll be off."

"Why, I'm very sorry, Mr. Wilson, very sorry, indeed, but you see—the fact is—well I can't do it because your father is not in business here any more. I'm employed by others."

"Not in business? What do you mean? Has he sold out? What—?" Wilson, staggered, was unable to frame the questions that rushed to his lips.

"I'm sorry, Mr. Wilson," said Sanders. "It is rather an involved matter, and doubtless your father will explain it to you when you see him. And now if you will excuse me, please, I must attend to some rather important business matters."

"Old Sanders" walked away, looking back at Wilson with that same expression of half embarrassment, half pity. Wilson, dazed, angry, and perplexed, went back to his hotel.

There was nothing left now but to get to Miquelon as quickly as possible. He had just about enough money left to finance the trip, and now that his plan to get more had failed, it would not do to dally in New

York. In anger he half decided to stay anyway, and, when his money was gone, telegraph to his father and tell him he he must send more. He abandoned this thought, however, when curiosity got the better of anger. Why had his father given up business? He left for Miquelon that night.

Travelling north, impatience aggravated his anger. He recounted his grievances to himself. First his father had spoiled his summer by sending for him. Then he had ordered him to pay Wembridge, thus putting a serious crimp in his bank roll. Then he had gone out of business, making it impossible for him to draw funds in New York. Wilson felt very much injured.

Brooding, he conceived an idea of making his father realize the enormity of his offence. He would arrive at Miquelon absolutely penniless. Actually, according to his calculations, he would have a few dollars left in his pocket, but these could easily be tossed overboard as the boat neared Miquelon. The dramatic possibilities of the idea seemed greater and greater as he considered it. Wilson Bersey, son of John

Bersey, comes home without a cent in his pocket. Millionaire's son has to shave the last penny to obey his father's orders. So he dramatized the scene, feeling already that he was something of a martyr, and picturing to himself the chagrin with which his father would learn of his financial status.

On the boat at last, with his passage paid and no more expenses to be incurred, Wilson took out his pocketbook. It contained a ten-dollar bill, a five-dollar bill, and a one-dollar bill. In his vest pocket was thirty-five cents in change. He considered the advisability of giving the money to one of the sailors on the boat, but decided against it lest his father should hear of his apparent generosity and thus lose the force of the dramatic climax. He stepped over to the rail of the boat, leaning nonchallantly, as though gazing at the churning water below, and dropped first the thirty-five cents, by way of experiment. Nobody seemed to notice this, and he felt it safe to proceed with the larger amount. He rolled the three bills into a tight wad, then glancing around again to make sure that he was unobserved, dropped them hastily into the sea. They floated for a moment beside the boat, blending with the green of the water, and then were lost to sight. Wilson, highly pleased with himself, strolled into the cabin.

Joe Kirkup was waiting at the dock when the boat arrived, his leathery, thatched face sober, his eyes melancholy. "Hello, Wilson," he said.

"Oh, hello," said Wilson, turning away from him to attend to his baggage.

"Never mind the baggage now," said Joe. "I'll attend to it later."

"Some things I want right away," Wilson said peevishly. Then he deliberated as to which bag to take to bear out his statement, as he had said this merely to show his independence. He disliked Joe, feeling that his intimate manner was unseemly in one whom he considered a mere servant, and he intended to show him that he would not be told what to do and what not to do.

"But your father is waiting for you," Joe urged.

"Let him wait," said Wilson. "If he was

so anxious to see me, why didn't he come down to meet me?"

"Why, you young fool," yelled Joe, aroused at this as no insult to himself could have aroused him, "don't you know that your father is dying while you stand there and act like an ornery hound?"

"Dying!" Wilson turned pale, and started to run toward the lodge. Joe followed. Even the terror that the word "dying" had produced within him, however, could not offset the life of ease Wilson had been living, and he soon had to slow down to a rapid walk to regain his breath. Then he started to run again, with Joe still at his heels. Thus they arrived at the lodge.

At the door Wilson hesitated. Never in his life had he been in such a state of unreasoning terror. Joe pushed open the door, and Wilson followed him inside, unconsciously stepping on tip-toes.

They approached the door of John Bersey's room. From within came the low whining of a dog. Joe Kirkup started at the sound, and shook his head. Softly he opened the door. John Bersey lay still as marble on the bed. The dog, Pieface, stood over him, whining low, realizing only that some mysterious metamorphosis had come over his master.

Joe Kirkup knelt by the side of the bed and listened for John Bersey's heartbeats, knowing as he did so that John Bersey's heart would beat no more.

"You're too late," he said.

Wilson Bersey slumped on the floor, fainting.

CHAPTER III

THE INHERITANCE

JOHN Bersey's funeral was a simple ceremony, held on the island; his body was buried in the little island cemetery. Joe Kirkup bore the expense from his own scanty savings, although he did not tell Wilson this. He did not dare to tell the boy the whole truth about things at once, fearing the effect of another shock added to that produced by his father's death.

Wilson, too dazed to reason, accepted Joe's explanation of the simple island funeral—that his father had wished it so, rather than having his body sent back to New York for a more impressive ceremony. He accepted, too, Joe's explanation of the absence of the dogs from the kennels—that his father had wished to see them safely sold and in good hands before he died. But by little words here and there, Joe tried to prepare Wilson to learn the truth. He failed, however, because nothing less than and out-and-out declaration of fact could have put into Wilson's mind the thought that his father had died in poverty. The idea was too grotesquely unreasonable to be born of hints and suggestions.

In the end, Joe had to leave it all to be told in a letter left by John Bersey for his son. It was the day after the funeral that the old caretaker called the boy to the room where his father had died, and produced an envelope from John Bersey's desk. Solemnly and silently he handed the envelope to Wilson, and then sat down to wait for him to read the enclosed message.

"My dear son," Wilson read, "I am writing this in case I should pass away before you arrive, although I fervently hope to see you once more before that happens.

"How can I tell you in a letter the terrible things that have happened. Yet I must, and I know no way except to speak out bluntly. I have lost everything—everything." (What horrible, ghastly joke was this? Wilson looked up at Joe for a sign, but Joe's face was utterly grave, and he nodded slowly, solemnly, pityingly. The boy read on, his face suddenly pale.)

"My business is gone; all my property is gone; this house in which I am dying is already owned by another; even the dogs in the kennels have been sold to satisfy my creditors. Oh, my boy, my boy!" (Wilson closed his eyes. The thing could not be true. It was too unreal. It was impossible. There must be something further down in the letter to change things around. He must read on.)

"You see what this means, Wilson. It means that I have nothing to leave you." (That was it. That was the fact that he had been trying to grasp. But it could not be. He, Wilson Bersey, not wealthy—with nothing, in fact? Oh, no. Yet, the picture of himself leaning over the railing and dropping a tightly-rolled wad into the green sea flashed back upon him, and he winced.)

"The bitter part of it is, my dear son, that I was trying to make your place in life more secure, and not being satisfied with what I had to give you, I tried to get more and lost what I had. Please try to believe that I was doing it for you, small consolation though that may be." (Reading this, Wilson felt a surge of anger against his father pass over him. The words which had been meant to soften him had just the opposite effect, and put the thought of blame into his mind. His father had ruined his life; that was it. For a moment he considered tearing up the hateful letter, without reading more, but the vague hope persisted that something alleviating might follow and compelled him to continue.)

"I said I had nothing to leave you, and yet I have something." (Ah, that was better.)

"Sometimes it has seemed to me, Wilson, that you did not share my love for dogs, but I know you have had other things to occupy your mind. But before I die I want to tell you that you will be making a big mistake if you fail to learn and profit by the heart and soul of a dog. A man can have no finer friend, no better teacher and counselor than his dog. I say this reverently, knowing that my life is soon to end." (Why all this talk? Why didn't the letter get on with the subject of the "something" which was to be left? Wilson wasted no thought on the advice, but read impatiently on.)

"And so, my boy, what I have to leave you may not seem very much. Had it been of great value, I could not have saved it from the wreck. But to me, it was just about my most precious possession. It can be so to you, if you will learn its value. Its monetary value is practically nothing, yet it is invaluable. All that I have to give you, then, is my favorite dog, Pieface."

There was one more paragraph, but Wilson did not read it. He merely glanced and saw that it was more talk about the nature of dogs and something about a father's love for his son. "Affectionately," John Bersey had signed himself, and Wilson, seeing that word, had felt that it was mockery. How could his father have had any affection for him and left him penniless? It was easy enough to write, "I did it for you," but what help was that? His father had ruined him; tricked him; led him to expect wealth, and then left him what? A miserable worthless dog.

Deliberately, bitterly, Wilson tore the

hateful letter into small bits, and dropped
the small bits to the floor. He was vaguely
aware of Joe Kirkup's eyes upon him as
he did this, but it did not matter. Nothing
mattered. He might as well be dead. He
sat immovable, trying to think, but his mind
was too full of bitterness against his father.
Tricked. Ruined.

"It broke his heart, boy," said Joe Kirkup, breaking his silence, and thinking of
John Bersey. " 'What will become of the
boy, Joe?' he asked me. And I told him,
'It'll be hard on him at first, maybe, John,'
says I, 'but he's your son, John, and he'll
come out right in the end.' So I told your
father, Wilson, and so I believe."

Wilson heard the old man's voice as
though in a dream, but the words meant
nothing to him. In the same half-compre-
hending way he was aware that Joe had
now risen from his chair, and was standing
over by the door.

"I don't know what you're thinking, Wilson," said Joe, as he stood with his hand
on the doorknob, "but I don't expect I can
be of much help to you right now, whatever it is." He opened the door, and the

dog, Pieface, scampered through it, into the room. "This is him," said Joe Kirkup, simply. "He can help you more than I can right now." He stepped out, and closed the door behind him.

Pieface looked at the closed door in disappointment. He had wanted to come in because Joe was there, and now that he was inside, Joe was outside. John Bersey was not here any more; that he knew. And he half realized the significance of that terrible stillness which had possessed his master the last time he saw him. He therefore looked to Joe now for companionship. This new young man, with whom he was now closed up in the room, he had not been able to classify yet in his mind.

He watched the door several minutes, thinking Joe might be teasing him and making him wait, but Joe did not return and the door did not open. Then he turned his attention to Wilson. He tipped up his nose and looked inquiringly at Wilson for a space of seconds. Then, with deliberate tread, he moved nearer, circled the chair, and sniffed of Wilson's trouser legs.

Wilson sat rigid. His eyes morosely followed the dog, but in no other way did he acknowledge his presence. Pieface sat down uncertainly at his feet. He shifted his fore-paws, considering the advisability of put-ting them up on Wilson's knees, thus forc· ing an acquaintanceship, but the youth's dis-couraging lack of interest seemed too much of a challenge to his pride, and he with-drew to an opposite corner and curled up as though for a nap. For a time he watched the still figure in the chair, but became tired at last and dozed.

He was awakened by Wilson's voice, and he looked around to see if Joe had returned to the room. He had not. The room was still occupied only by Wilson and himself. Wilson must be talking to him, therefore, he decided. He rose with dignity, and stood with ears pricked up to catch what was being said, but he could make nothing of it. He could not even interpret the tone of voice although he knew that it was not a tone of a happy shade. Then he heard his name mentioned, and emitted a short bark in response, but the words that followed were as unintelligible as those which had gone before.

"So this is my inheritance," Wilson had been saying. "This mutt! Pieface!" (It was here that the dog had barked, and if he had been better acquainted with Wilson's voice he probably would have barked louder and longer, recognizing the note of deep scorn and bitterness in which his name was spoken.) "No money. Nothing. Only this mutt, and what did he think I wanted of that? Not even a show dog that I could sell—" Wilson fell into silence again, finding words of little use in relieving his feelings.

Pieface, wondering what was the trouble, marched across the room and stood again at Wilson's feet, looking up. Wilson met his gaze. His entire world was at his feet. A new feeling of terror seemed to possess him as he realized this fact. He rose quickly, uttering something between a moan and an unexpressed curse, stepped by the dog, and walked quickly to the door. Pieface followed at his heels, glad to see that the door was going to be opened at last, allowing him to seek more congenial companionship.

But Wilson, opening the door, stepped

through it quickly and slammed it shut behind him, leaving the dog shut up inside.
"Stay in there," he said, half screaming,
"and I hope I may never see you again."

He ran at top speed down the stairs, out
the door, and into a field, where he flung
himself at full length on the ground and
sobbed like a child. He sobbed not for the
loss of his father, but for the loss of his
wealth.

Pieface scratched at the door, wondering
more than ever about this strange young
man.

CHAPTER IV

CAST UPON THE WATERS

WILSON slept that night in the lodge, though he slept fitfully, waking every now and again and realizing that the lodge was not his; that he did not belong there; that he did not belong anywhere. During one of these wakeful spells he heard Pieface moving about in an adjoining room. Joe Kirkup had released the dog from the room where Wilson had imprisoned him, and he had attempted to attach himself to Joe again, but the old caretaker, determined that John Bersey's last wish should be carried out, had brought him back to the lodge and left him to get acquainted with his new master.

Hearing him move around now, his new master felt a strong desire to get up and throw him out of the house, and would have done so had not the comfort of the bed been too strong as a counter-attraction.

The dog was his to abuse as long and as often as he saw fit, he argued to himself, but he did not know how long he would be able to sleep in a good bed—he who had never had to give beds a thought before.

But as he lay there, thinking such thoughts, Pieface became more and more a hateful figure in his mind. His wrath began to turn from his father, against whom it was useless, to the dog, on which he could give it vent. Gradually Pieface took form as the symbol of his misfortune. This dog—this utterly worthless dog—was his only possession, and he despised him because of his worthlessness.

Then, letting his mind wander, he again saw himself as he had leaned over the rail and dropped the wad of bills into the sea. What a failure that climax had been! Yet, queerly enough, he still got some thrill of self-admiration out of the memory of the act. It still seemed somehow heroic, when on the verge of pennilessness, wilfully to make the state absolute. For instance, now—

He sat up in bed with a start, as the idea struck him. What if he should do with Pieface as he had done with the money? Would that not be snapping his fingers under the nose of Fate? With one masterly stroke it would give him revenge against this beastly dog (which now, for some illogical reason, he considered the cause as well as the personification of his troubles) and make him a hero, in his own eyes, at least, who dared to spurn the measly gift of Fortune.

Now he listened with a malicious sort of pleasure for the sound of the dog in the next room, and was disappointed when he heard nothing, Pieface having settled down to sleep. Schemes, half-formed, for the accomplishment of his purpose filled Wilson's mind until, at last, he fell asleep again.

He arose early and dressed. Pieface, hearing him stirring, was waiting when Wilson, following out the plans made in the night, greeted the dog with a pat on the head, as though he had at last decided to become friendly. Pieface, always in search of friends, was delighted.

The lodge was deserted except for these two, the servants having been paid off and sent away some time before; and Joe Kirk-

up, who had been acting as chef and handy
man, as well as John Bersey's nurse, having gone back to his own little home. Therefore Wilson was obliged to prepare his own
breakfast for the first time in his life, and
he went into the kitchen to see what he
could do along that line. Pieface, also
hungry, followed. For himself Wilson
found an orange, which required only to be
peeled and was thereby within the range of
possibilities. He found some meat in the
ice chest, and tossed it on the floor for
Pieface, who took full advantage of it and
became correspondingly more favorably dis-
posed toward Wilson.

"Have a good meal, Pieface," said Wilson, "you'll never have another."

Pieface obeyed gladly, although there was
something about Wilson's new tone of apparent friendliness that was not quite con-
vincing. Yet he had never had reason to
mistrust people, and so his feeling toward
the youth was one of curiosity rather than
mistrust. After all, he decided, Wilson's
attitude to-day was a decided improvement
over that of the preceding days, and he
would accept it as such—particularly as he

was being fed one of the choicest pieces of meat he had ever eaten.

Breakfast over, Wilson went outside, calling Pieface to follow. He walked rapidly down the road to the shore. Pieface ran, now ahead of him, now at his heels, as he had used to do when John Bersey took him out over the island.

In the days when Wilson had been a regular summer resident of the island, his father had bought him a sailing dory, in which the boy had spent many pleasant hours. He did not know whether this had been sold with his father's property or not, but he headed for the place where it had always been kept. It was in the usual place.

"Get in, Pieface," said Wilson, pointing to the boat. The dog, having often sailed with Joe Kirkup, and less frequently with John Bersey, gladly availed himself of the invitation. Sailing was one of his favorite sports. He therefore jumped in, ran to the bow of the boat, and took his favorite position with his forepaws up on the rail of the dory.

Wilson busied himself for a few minutes

getting everything in readiness, then shoved off the dory and hopped in. A little way out from shore he set the sails, heading the dory straight out toward the wide Atlantic. Then he sat back, steering steadily and let the breeze carry them oceanward.

Pieface, getting more or less drenched with spray, gave up his place at the bow and decided to come back and see how his new friend was getting on. He picked his way gingerly back to the stern, and looked up into Wilson's face. But Wilson was once more the silent, aloof person of the day before. His friendliness had accomplished his purpose, and he saw no benefit to be derived from further deception. He looked at the dog with no attempt to disguise his hatred. But he said nothing.

At first this puzzled Pieface, and he cocked his head inquiringly. But then he remembered the breakfast Wilson had given him, the morning pat on the head and the apparently friendly words, and decided that his new friend was merely given to moods when he did not want to be bothered. So he remained quiet, watching the water slip by.

Out beyond, the masts of fishing schooners could be seen here and there. Still further out, a trail of smoke in the sky showed the course of some hurrying steamer. And the shore line dropped farther and farther back behind them.

Wilson, dramatizing in his mind the thing he was bent on doing, was enjoying in advance a sort of bitter pleasure. Self-pity having overcome every other emotion within him, he felt that it was a heroic thing to drown a dog, when that dog was one's only possession. He was entirely too self-centered to have any particular feeling for dogs, and for that matter, he thought of Pieface less as a dog than as a piece of property. Thus he did not think of what he was about to do as killing a dog, but as destroying his only piece of property. Fortunately the property was not very valuable so he could indulge his flair for heroics without any appreciable personal loss.

He pictured himself going back to the island and telling Joe Kirkup that Pieface was at the bottom of the ocean. What a blow that would be to Joe, and how he would delight in seeing the old man suffer.

(Wilson was such a thorough misanthrope by this time that making others suffer seemed the biggest pleasure in life.) Yet he knew that he would never have the courage to tell Joe Kirkup he had killed Pieface, even as he pictured himself doing it. He knew too well that Joe's punishment for such a deed would be swift and sure. Joe was another of those absurd men who looked upon dogs as demigods. Oh, well, he would have the personal satisfaction of knowing what he had done, even if he had to forego the pleasure of letting Joe know about it, too.

"Pieface," he said suddenly.

The dog hastened to respond to his call, and stood at his feet.

"I'm going to drop you overboard," Wilson announced.

Pieface wagged his tail.

"Stop wagging your tail, you fool," shouted Wilson, irritated.

Pieface, thinking this must be some new game, wagged the harder, and barked heartily to make the fun more furious.

"Shut up," yelled Wilson, suddenly finding himself doubtful whether or not he would dare to go through with his plans. Just what it was that made him afraid, he did not know, but something inside him seemed to be telling him that he could not do it.

The dog continued to bark, mock-ferociously, and even jumped up and pawed at Wilson with his forepaws. Wilson pushed him roughly down. But even this rough usage failed to discourage the fun-starved dog, who took the push as part of the game, and crouched back in the bottom of the boat, simulating ferociousness still. He growled, shook his head and bared his teeth, waiting for Wilson's next move to prompt further action in the game.

Wilson knew the dog was playing, but as he looked at him he found himself wondering what would happen if this play were in earnest. Suppose Pieface should find out what he planned to do, and should endeavor to defend himself. Suppose, as he crouched there, he were waiting for a good opportunity to sink those bared teeth into his enemy. Suppose—

But even as Wilson speculated, Pieface decided to push the game along a little faster. He emitted a few extra-sharp barks, and then leaped forward.

Wilson rose in his place. The thoughts that had been passing through his mind as vague suppositions suddenly seemed to become actualities as he saw the dog flying toward him. His overwrought reason refused to function, and in those few seconds he firmly believed that the dog had found him out, and was coming at him with the desire to maim and kill.

He raised his arm with a violence that only terror could have inspired. His subconscious purpose in this was to protect himself from the dog which he thought was attacking him. But as he brought it up, the dog was in mid-air, expecting only to come in mild contact with his body. Instead, the arm took the dog by surprise, struck him just under his forelegs and toppled him over backwards—into the sea.

Wilson saw the dog fall with surprise. Realizing suddenly that Pieface had only been playing, else he would not have been bowled over so easily, his first impulse was to reach over and pull him back into the dory. But then he remembered that it was for this very thing that he had brought him out here. He had intended just to pick him up and drop him overboard, but now the same end had been accomplished in another way. Well, so be it.

He made a wide circle with the dory, and headed it back toward the island. He could see Pieface swimming around where he had gone overboard. He steered the boat close to the dog and came alongside him.

"This is the end of you, Pieface," he shouted.

Pieface swam hard, trying to keep up with the boat, but steadily it passed him. He wasted no breath, but his eyes pleaded for an end to thus cruel joke. It was too much like reality to see the boat pulling away from him. It was just as though Wilson did not intend to come back and pull him into the boat again.

The dory pulled farther and farther away. Pieface slowed down in his swimming. Then it was true. The boat was not coming back. He had been abandoned away out here in the ocean.

Wilson, looking back from the dory, saw

the little speck of white which was Pieface
turn and move the other way—out to sea.

He tried to feel again the heroic thrill
that he had preconceived but somehow it
had become converted into a cold chill.

CHAPTER V

CAP'N Gus Spokes, skipper of the fishing schooner "Alice M.," paced up and down the deck of that trim little craft, bemoaning the fate that ruled over fishermen. Three weeks ago he had brought the vessel into the fishing grounds about four miles off the coast of Miquelon, and prepare to haul in a cargo of fish. But day after day the fish had eluded him, and after three weeks of futile fishing he had hardly been able to cover the bottom of his hold.

He gazed sadly down into the green water. "Ain't they no fish in this here ocean?" he demanded, eloquently if ungrammatically. The lap-lapping of the waves against the side of the ship was his only answer. He tamped some tobacco into a stubby pipe, clutched the pipe between his teeth, and resumed his pacing up and down the deck.

By all rights he should have had his hold full to overflowing by this time, and be on his way back to Portland. Cap'n Gus knew fishing and he knew the fishing grounds. Twenty years of fishing out of Portland had developed in him that instinct which guides the fisherman to the place where the fish are abundant. And it was that sense which had told him to bring his vessel out here off the coast of Miquelon. But the fish were not playing the game. They were not here, and Cap'n Gus was checkmated.

"Can't go back to Portland with this little mess o' fish," he grumbled to himself. "Ain't enough to pay for the salt they're stowed in. Still the'ain't much use hangin' out here much longer. I dunno—" He spat meditatively into the ocean.

The men moved lackadaisically to their tasks. "Trawlin' for fish where th'ain't no fish," Bill Johnson expressed it. The other men grinned at Bill's drollery, but half-heartedly. They were wearying of this profitless game.

Cap'n Gus continued his meditative pacing, up and down, up and down. He leaned against the rail, and gazed absently out over the water, trying to reach a decision. His eye followed a sea gull, hovering over the water in the distance. Or was it a sea gull? Maybe it was just a box or something, drifting. A white cardboard box, or a bunch of paper. Or something. Oh, well, what difference did it make? There was one thing it wasn't, and that was a school of fish. He withdrew his gaze.

Up and down, up and down. Fishermen's luck! Three weeks of fishing, and not enough fish to pay for the salt. Should he give it up? "Ain't they no fish in this here ocean?"

Another disconsolate pause by the rail, and his eye sought out again the floating thing out in the water. It seemed to be floating nearer the ship, getting bigger as the perspective decreased. Funny how it could make so much progress, Cap'n Gus thought. It was almost as though the thing were swimming. Yet it was plain now that it was not a sea gull. Funny.

He watched it with more interest, letting his fishing troubles be submerged for the time being. Could it be something swimming? It seemed absurd away out here. Still—

"Hey, Bill," shouted Cap'n Gus. "C'm'-ere a minute."

Bill came, glad of the opportunity to change his occupation temporarily.

Cap'n Gus pointed. "See that white thing out there?"

"Piece of paper, ain't it?" said Bill.

"I dunno. Thought it was at first, but blamed if I don't think the thing is swim-min'. See—it is swimmin', ain't it?"

"Might be," said Bill. "Still, it don't seem likely. What d'ye suppose would be swimmin' this far out?"

"Dunno," said Cap'n Gus, absorbed in watching, "but I'll lay ye a bet that 'tis.

The two men stood still, watching. It is not often that the ocean produces any-thing more interesting than a storm.

"Does seem to be swimmin', don't it?" said Bill, at length.

"Fetch my glass, Bill," said the cap'n. "Blamed if it don't look like a dog. I don't suppose it could be, though."

Bill hastened after the glass, though re-luctantly.

"Sure does look like a dog," Cap'n Gus muttered. "Blamed if it don't."

He seized the glass excitedly when Bill returned, adjusted it to his eye, and focused it on the object of interest.

"H'm, well I'll be blamed," he muttered.

"What is it? Is it a dog?" Bill was impatient for news.

Cap'n Gus adjusted the glass more to his liking. "I certainly will be blamed," said he.

"Is it a dog? What is it?"

"What do you know about that?" said the cap'n, eager, now that his own curiosity was satisfied, to work Bill up to the highest pitch of interest in order to make the climax the more effective.

"I don't know nothin' about it yet," said Bill. "What is it?"

"It's a dog," pronounced Cap'n Gus, as though no such possibility had been mentioned previously. He handed the glass to Bill, and the latter looked for himself.

"Is, ain't it?" he confirmed.

The two men looked at each other in puzzlement, then looked out again at the dog. It was coming steadily nearer to the ship, and was easily discernible as a dog now with the naked eye. The skipper called other members of his crew to share the diversion. Each was so amazed that he readily admitted never having seen such a thing happen before—which is an unusual admission for a seasoned seafaring man.

"Lower a dory," ordered the skipper; "there's goin' to be a rescue this day." He chose Bill and one other to be the rescuers.

The boat was lowered, and the two fishermen descended into it and rowed out to meet the swimming dog. The dog's progress was slower now than it had been when he was first sighted. His feet were paddling mechanically, but heavily. He seemed to hold his nose up only by a strong effort. Yet at the sight of the approaching dory, he seemed to gain fresh strength, and paddled gamely on to meet it.

Bill leaned over the side of the boat as they reached the dog, and his companion poised the oars.

"Aboard ye come, mate," said Bill, reaching a pair of powerful arms around the dog's middle, and hoisting him in.

The dog looked up at his rescuer a moment with grateful, tired eyes. Then he sank down in the boat with a sigh. One little ineffectual attempt he made to shake the water from his coat, after the manner of dogs, but he was too completely exhausted for this formality, and lay dripping in the bottom of the dory.

A more bedraggled, hopeless-looking dog than this one would be hard to imagine. Yet the men looked at him with unconcealed admiration.

"That-there's a dog what is a dog," uttered Bill, reverently.

"Swimmin' all that way," exclaimed the other, wondering as he spoke where it was that the dog had started his strange swim.

They remained silent then, while they rowed back to the schooner, as though the dripping dog were some sacred, awesome thing in whose presence speech was profane. The dog lay perfectly motionless, except when a spasmodic shiver set the water dripping faster from his soaking, white coat. He was still panting for breath after his long exertion, but after a few minutes he began to show the returning power of his lungs by emitting a strange noise that was half a groan and half a grateful sigh. So they drew up alongside the schooner.

Cap'n Gus and the other men had been watching the proceedings from the rail with all the excitement of schoolboys at a football game. And now, as the dory came alongside, they lowered a basket on a rope.

"Put him in the basket; put him in the basket," yelled Cap'n Gus. It was perfectly obvious what the basket was for, but the skipper was so excited that he had to shout directions, even though they were unnecessary.

Bill did as directed, and the dog was hauled aboard. Up by the forecastle a bed had been prepared for him, with as many soft bits of cloth as were available, and there he was transported, basket and all. Lifted from the basket to the bed, he stood uncertainly on his feet for a moment, then with a great effort satisfied his conscience by a determined shake of his body which produced a momentary shower bath for the men who stood nearest him. Then he settled down on the impromptu bed and closed his eyes, uttering again that half groan, half sigh, which best expressed his feelings.

"A bull terrier, and a good one," pronounced the skipper, surveying him with the eye of authority. "Now where do you suppose he came from?"

None answered the unanswerable.

Suddenly the skipper turned from his meditative survey of the exhausted dog "Cook!" he shouted. "Food and drink for the animal. Would you have him die on our hands just when we've rescued him?"

The cook hastened below and quickly returned with a pan of the choicest scraps his larder afforded and another pan of fresh water. The dog bestirred himself as these were set down before him; opened his eyes, and ate ravenously. Then, with great content, he settled back in his rags and slept. Cap'n Gus threw a pea-jacket over him, and signalled for the men to leave him to his well-earned slumber. The dog snored, twitched a little and occasionally made that strange sighing noise which indicated that even in his sleep he was still living through his strange experiences of the day.

All the rest of the day and all night he

slept, but in the morning, with the first stirring of the cook in the galley below, he was on his feet, staring with bewildered eyes at his unfamiliar surroundings. It was as though he had just awakened from a horrible nightmare, and at first he thought that was what had happened, but as he looked at the bed where he had slept and the empty pan that had contained food, he knew that some of his nightmare, at least had been actuality. Having settled this point to his satisfaction, he wondered how one went about it to get something to eat in such a place as this.

From the galley came the unmistakable odor of food. He trotted in that direction and paused, as he poked a questioning nose through the hatch. The cook was busy over the stove, and did not see him. He thought of dashing down and seizing some food behind the cook's back, but the thought died almost as soon as it was born. This cook was the man who had brought him food during that nightmare. Therefore he was a friend, and to be treated as such. The dog barked to notify the cook of his presence.

The cook jumped, but then remembering, turned and grinned up at the dog.

"Well, sir," said he, "so you're up and about this mornin'? Hungry as a crew o' good-for-nothin' fishermen, too, I'll bet. Hey?"

The dog barked again, by way of reply.

"Well, come down here then," said the cook, clapping his hands together to show the meaning of his invitation, "and I'll see what we can do about it."

The dog hastily availed himself of the invitation, and the cook tossed some pieces of fish into a corner, and stood watching and admiring the dog as he ate.

"Some dog," he said to himself, and reluctantly turned back to his stove as he heard the voices of the "crew of good-for-nothin' fishermen."

It was later than usual when the men started at their daily tasks that morning, for they had to take time to admire the dog fully, stroke him, play with him, and tell one another all over again how peculiar it was that he should have come to them out of the sea. But when they did get to work on the trawls, they received another surprise. For they began to haul in fish—not just a few scattering fish as they had been doing for three weeks, but great quantities of fish.

"It's the dog," they told one another, "He brought us luck." And they half believed it, being, like most fishermen, inclined to superstition. Some of them recalled old stories of fishermen who always took dogs to sea with them to assure good luck to the voyage, and of the remarkable bits of bad luck encountered when the dogs were temporarily ashore. Even Cap'n Gus, who prided himself on being superior to his men in intellect, was not prepared to deny outright the luck-bringing quality of the dog.

"He ain't doin' us no harm, anyway," he vouchsafed.

They talked it all over as they were dressing down the fish that night, and the dog, having been well fed by the cook, did not offer to interfere with the work, but sat and watched proceedings with great interest. He sensed that he was the subject of conversation, and he knew that he was among friends. He enjoyed himself immensely.

When the dressing down was finished, the men gathered around the dog in an admiring circle. The dog strolled from one to another, receiving a commendatory pat on the head or a playful chuck under the chin.

"C'm'ere, you ole sea dog," said Bill Johnson. "It's time I put ye to bed."

Cap'n Gus, who had been standing just outside the circle of men, stepped forward.

"We thank you kindly, Bill," said he, "but you don't need to bother yourself. Me and the sea dog will sleep in the cabin this night."

The skipper snapped his fingers, and the dog followed, wagging his tail as though he understood the honor that was paid him.

"Don't you tell them lubbers I told you," whispered Cap'n Gus to the dog in the privacy of the cabin, "but you're worth the whole lot of 'em on this bo't."

Bill Johnson, getting ready to turn in for the night, yelled out to his companions: "Like to see anybody get that dog away from the ole man now. There'd be a murder."

The men chuckled.

"Some dog," they murmured.

CHAPTER VI

BAD BUSINESS

WILSON Bersey, back on the island, was a prey to conflicting emotions. He had thought that if he threw Pieface into the sea to die it would be a balm to his feelings. But now that it had been done, the effect was quite the opposite. The pleading look in the dog's eyes when he last saw him remained in his memory, and brought to him the realization that Pieface had been a living creature, with feelings like his own. Try as he would, he could not regain his old impersonal attitude. He had thought he was casting away a useless thing; whereas now he knew that he had taken the life of a dog. And he could not overcome the self-contempt and self-hatred that was within him.

And yet, despite this belated change of heart in one respect, Wilson was still too much of a spoiled, selfish, and disappointed youth to undergo a general change. That unreasoning bitterness toward his father still remained; and there remained, too, the feeling of bitterness toward life in general which necessarily followed upon the loss of all his better nature.

The change that had come over him, then, was merely an addition of himself to his list of hates. Before, he had thought well of nobody and nothing but himself. Now he discovered that he himself had done a contemptible thing, and he could not longer think well even of himself. Life was utterly black.

He had not gone back to the lodge after returning to the island in his dory, but had remained down by the shore. He had sat and looked out to sea, visioning Pieface struggling against death in that boundless ocean and finally sinking down, down, down. Several times he had been on the point of shoving off the dory and returning to the spot where he had last seen the dog, on the forlorn chance that he might still be swimming out there, but each time he told himself that it was no use. Pieface was dead. He had killed him. He wanted to cry like a little child, but no tears came and he was only so much the more miserable.

That night he slept in the dory—or tried to sleep. He had not eaten anything all day, except that one orange in the morning, but somehow it did not seem to matter. If he could only cry. And at last, as he lay in the bottom of the dory, the tears came to his eyes, and he sobbed until he fell asleep. And he dreamed that he was hungry, and that Pieface was bringing him food and watching him while he ate it.

When he awoke in the morning, he instinctively looked around him for the dog, the dream still lingering as a reality. But then he realized that the only true part of it was his hunger, which would no longer be denied. He rubbed some of the cold sea water over his face, and set out for Joe Kirkup's house. He knew that Joe would not let him starve.

The old man appeared relieved when Wilson appeared at the door. He was just about to eat his own breakfast, but he gave it to Wilson instead, and got more for himself.

"Where in the world have you been?" he

demanded, after Wilson had eaten ravenously. "I looked all over the island for you,
almost, last night."

"I wanted to be alone," said Wilson.

The old man nodded.

"Where's Pieface?"

"I—I don't—I thought he was with
you," lied Wilson.

"That's funny. I thought he was with
you. Well, he must be around somewhere."

Joe sat quietly for a few minutes, looking out of the window; then, without chang-
ing his gaze, he said. "I suppose you've
been laying out your course?"

"I don't know what to do," said Wilson.

"I suppose you've got a little money?"

"No." (Again Wilson saw himself dropping his money into the sea, and, as though
it were a connected action, he saw the
pleading eyes of Pieface looking at him
from the water.)

"Well, now, I could let you have a little
money, if you should want to go to any
of your friends," suggested Joe.

Wilson recoiled at the thought of going
to any of his friends. They were all wealthy;
he was penniless—and he remembered

the contempt he had always felt for those who were not wealthy. Most of his friends, he knew, felt the same way, and he did not propose to make himself an object for their sneers.

"No," he said.

"I just as soon let you have it as not," said Joe, misunderstanding the motive behind the refusal of his offer.

"I don't want to go to my friends," said Wilson.

"Well, then, perhaps you might like enough money to go to New York and see some of your father's business friends. I suppose, after all, that would be better, then you could get a job."

Wilson pictured the job that he would be likely to get. A messenger boy, probably. Men like old Sanders would order him about, and he would have to cross the street when he saw any of his old friends, lest they recognize him and laugh at his occupation. No, he would never do it.

"No," he said, again.

"I just as soon let you have it as not," Joe repeated.

"I don't want to work in New York."

"Well, you're welcome to stay right here just as long as you want to."

"I don't want to stay here."

Joe scratched his head, then tugged at his whiskers, perplexed.

"Guess I'll go see if I can find Pieface anywheres around," he said. "Let me know if I can help you any."

He went out, shaking his bewildered old head at the door as he closed it behind him, and left Wilson sitting glumly at the barren breakfast table.

The boy arose, walked to the window and stood staring out. From where he stood he could see a schooner tied up to the freight dock, and men busily loading her.

"Rum-runner," he thought idly, knowing that the little French island was a favorite storage point for the modern outlaws of the sea, and that most of the freighters that came in and out of its harbor were engaged in carrying liquor.

He turned away from the window, and walked around the room. He had never had to give much thought to the future, and it was difficult to do so now. In the back of his head the two courses which Joe had suggested had been forming for a day or two, but now that Joe had put them bluntly before him, he had rejected them. What then, could he do?

Wilson's unfortunate bringing-up had engendered in him a contempt for those who had to work for the good things of life. Yet he knew that he must become one of them.

"Very well," he said softly to himself, "Then I will work at something that will bring me a lot of money quickly—and I don't care what it is."

All of which was very easy to say, but not so easy to put into operation. The get-rich-quick occupations, even when moral scruples are laid aside, are not so easy to find. Wilson sat down and thought and thought, but failed to summon up even the faintest glimmering of an idea.

Angrily he got up and walked to the window again, and stood glowering out. Miquelon was not the place to start to get rich quick, anyway, he decided. All folks did here was to fish and run rum.

Rum-running? Those fellows did make a lot of money, though. Or, at least, he had heard fabulous fortunes made by them. Why should he not make a fortune the same way? Yet it was pretty dangerous. He looked over at the dock. The men were still busy, loading the rum ship. He wondered—

A rum-runner. An outlaw. What a low and ugly occupation for the son of John Bersey! Yet he owed his father nothing, or so he thought in his ungrateful bitterness. And as for what the world might think—it need never know. He would make his fortune and then quit. If he was caught —well, he would take the chance. He despised himself for the decision, but he made it. He failed to realize that it was his own opinion of himself that really mattered, rather than the opinion of the world.

Fearing that he would lose his determination if he delayed and thought about it longer, he seized his cap and hurried out the door, walking with quick steps in the direction of the dock. As he walked, the thought of Pieface returned to him. Those pleading eyes. First he had thrown his money overboard; then his dog. What was he about to throw overboard now? Was it something that would haunt him as the eyes of the dog were haunting him? He broke into a trot, hoping to shake off the memory of the deserted dog, but the very sounds made by his feet as they met the solid earth beneath him seemed to say, "Pieface drowned; Pieface drowned; Pieface drowned."

Arriving at the dock, he stood and watched operations a few minutes. Then he approached a sailor, who had paused to light his pipe, and tapped him on the arm.

"Where is this ship going?" he asked.

"Bermuda," answered the seaman, shortly."

Wilson knew that the ship might sail for Bermuda officially, but that it would never arrive there unless it failed to dispose of its cargo somewhere along the American coast. He smiled wisely, and the sailor, winking, started to walk away.

"Who is the captain?" asked Wilson, following him.

"What d'yer wanter know for?"

"I want a job."

"Huh? Yer mean yer wanter ship on this tub?"

"Yes."

"Don't be silly, kid. The revenooers eat kids like you."

"Don't be silly, yourself. I'm no kid, and I know what I want."

"Oh, well, it's O. K. with me. You got a husky build on yer, even if yer do look kinder young and soft. That's the cap over there. Name's Smith."

The sailor pointed to a little, wizened-up runt of a man, who stood at the end of the dock, chewing a big black cigar and watching everything that was going on with little eyes like pig eyes. Wilson approached him.

"Cap'n Smith?"

The little pig eyes focused themselves on the questioner, but the little man said nothing. His gaze was sullen and baleful, and Wilson felt uncomfortable under it, especially as the thin lips of the man remained tight closed.

"My name is Bersey."

With a gesture as though of great weariness and intolerance, the skipper of the rum ship removed the cigar from his mouth.

"Well?" he said.

"I would like to join your crew, sir."

The skipper moved his head negatively the fraction of an inch, replaced the cigar between his yellow teeth, and turned his back on the applicant. Wilson was baffled for the moment by this summary refusal of his services, but he was determined not to give up his questionable career so easily before it even was started. He stepped around and confronted the skipper again.

"Couldn't you find a place to use me somewhere, sir?" he asked.

Again the almost imperceptible wagging of the head, and again Captain Smith turned his back. And again Wilson walked around to face him.

"See here, Cap'n," said Wilson, "I want to make some money. I know you are a rum-runner, and I want to join you. Why won't you take me on?"

The skipper removed the cigar again with great deliberation. The pig eyes looked the youth up and down for several seconds.

"Men in my business can't be bothered with crazy kids. I wouldn't take you as a gift. Now git."

When he turned this time, he walked

rapidly away. A gaunt mongrel dog leaped from a bale of straw nearby and followed him. At the other end of the dock the skipper stopped, turned, and stood fondling the dog. His eyes looked less like pig eyes, and his face lost its appearance of chronic sullenness and acquired a half-grin.

And Wilson, watching, was not thinking for the moment of his failure to be accepted as a rum runner.

"Even that little beast of a man," he muttered to himself, "wouldn't drown a dog."

CHAPTER VII

SHIP AHOY

AFTER leaving the dock Wilson walked slowly up to the lodge that had been his father's. Already it seemed a strange, unfriendly place, although once it had been one of his homes. He admitted himself with a key that Joe had given him when he first arrived, and went to the room that had been his own. There he picked up whatever he had unpacked from his bags and repacked them. Then, with a bag in each hand, he left the house. A little shudder worked up and down his spine as he slammed the door behind him. The last time he left this house it had been with Pieface.

He marched through the dust with the bags, stopping now and then to rest. His arms and hands were not accustomed to such burdens. Eventually, however, he arrived at Joe Kirkup's house, pushed open

the unlocked door with his foot, and entered.
He deposited the bags in a corner, and sank
into a chair, weary. Then an envelope,
propped up against the sugar bowl on the
table, caught his eye. Leaning forward, he
read the words on the envelope: "Wilson
Bersey, care of J. Kirkup." It bore a New
York postmark.

He reached the letter, tore it open and
read:

"Dear Sir,
In disposing of the goods in the New
York house of John Bersey, we have, according to instructions, saved out certain
personal belongings of yours, mainly clothing. These are at present stored in our
warehouse, but as we do no private storage
business, we should be glad to have instructions from you as to their disposition.

Unless we are otherwise instructed within the next few days, we shall ship them
to you at your present address, charges collect.
                    Yours truly,
                    Verburg & Glutz."

"Ghouls," he muttered, "Ship them collect for all I care; then try and collect."

He half smiled at his own bravado, but

the smile died as he crammed the letter
into his pocket. It was another reminder of
his utter homelessness. At times he had
not been able to convince himself that the
house in New York would not be open to
him if he chose to go there. But this
letter convinced him finally. He could see,
in his mind's eye, the moving vans backed
up to the door; the familiar furniture being
moved away to some dusty auction room;
the servants turning for a last look at the
old establishment, as they toted their lug-
gage out through the servants entrance;
the walls bare, the house empty, waiting
for its next occupants.

He must do something—anything. But
what? He cupped his head in his hands and
tried to think, but his mind was a muddle.

It was thus that Joe found him a half
hour later. But Joe's mind, too, was pre-
occupied now, and his face showed signs
of worry.

"You seen Pieface yet?" he asked.

"No."

"Sure?"

"Certainly I'm sure," Wilson snapped.

"Dog-gone funny, that's all I can say,"

Joe mused. "I've hunted everywhere for him, and I can't find him. He was never away like this before."

Wilson deigned no reply, but he had to smile at Joe's choice of a qualifying adjective. "Dog-gone funny."

Joe saw the smile, without knowing its cause, and it added to suspicions that he already was beginning to harbor.

"See here, Wilson," said the old man, "I promised your father that I would do what I could to look out for you and Pieface." He emphasized the "and Pieface." "Now I dunno as I'm much good at looking out for you, but leastways I aim to look out for the dog, specially as you don't seem to be paying any attention to him. Now I ask you again, are you sure you ain't seen him?"

"I told you I hadn't seen him. And what if I had? He's mine, isn't he?"

"Nobody really owns a good dog until the dog owns him," pronounced Joe. "And I'm beginning to wonder if you'll ever be fit to own a dog."

"Bunk," said Wilson.

"All right, Wilson. All right. I want to

help you if I can, and I don't want to make things any harder for you than they are already. But I just can't help mentioning that Pieface couldn't disappear off this island all by himself, and if I should ever find that you'd done anything—"

He left it at that and went out to continue his search. After a little while, Wilson also went out, but not to search. He went down to the shore and lay there. In the early afternoon and again in the early evening he went back to Joe's house and found himself something to eat. The second time he found Joe there. The old man watched him somberly as he went to the kitchen, but spoke not so much as a word of greeting. All Wilson stopped to say was, "I'm hungry," as he hastened to avoid Joe's suspicious eyes.

But as he came out of the kitchen, and started to make for the door again, Joe stopped him with a curt "Wilson."

"Yes?" said Wilson.

"I haven't found Pieface yet."

"Is that so? What could have become of him?"

"I wonder," said Joe, but his tone implied something more specific.

Wilson bolted through the door, and ran again down to the shore. He did not return until he knew that Joe would be in bed. Then he crept in and threw himself on the cot. He was thoroughly afraid now, knowing that Joe was suspicious of him, and he did not even take off his shoes lest he be unable to flee if the occasion arose.

He lay on the cot trying to decide what his next move should be. He must get away from here; that was sure. If another day passed and Pieface was still missing— as he would be—there was no telling what Joe might do to him. If he only could have persuaded that rum-runner to take him aboard. The vessel would be sailing in the morning.

The plan evolved itself in his head slowly. At first he thought of running out now and trying to stow away in the rum ship, but he knew that chances of getting aboard were not good. They watched things pretty closely on that kind of vessel. He considered making another attempt to persuade the skipper in the morning. But the memory of those pig eyes of scorn and the impatient turning on the heel was not encouraging.

It was another memory that first suggested the plan—the memory of that rat-faced skipper suddenly smiling with affection as he fondled a gaunt mongrel dog. He had thought as he watched the man that even he, low as he was, would not have drowned a dog. Probably he would not drown a man, either, unless he had some particular reason to want to get rid of him. Probably he would not even let a man drown, if he could do anything to prevent it. It was on this foundation that he built his scheme.

At last he slept fitfully, but at the first sound of Joe dressing in the adjoining room, he jumped from the cot, ran into the kitchen and seized a handful of doughnuts, and then ran out into the cool morning air. He made his way at once to the dock, and waited for signs of action, munching his doughnuts as he waited. Presently men began to come and go. He watched until he saw the sailor with whom he had talked yesterday, and accosted him.

"When are you sailing?" he asked.

"Couple a hours, I guess. The cap wouldn' take yer would he?"

"No."

"Tough. Well, so long."

"Good-by."

Wilson turned and walked rapidly to the place where his sailing dory was beached. Shoving it off, he jumped in, adjusted the sail and proceeded, as he had done two days before, out to sea. It was not a pleasant sail, for he was following almost the same route that he had taken on the day which now rankled in his memory, and he lowered his sail at very nearly the same spot where Pieface had gone overboard. He tried not to think of that, but he might as well have tried to stop the waves from rolling.

He drifted idly about for a half hour or more, then unfurled his sail again, and sailed out a bit, tacked around and came back, then out again, then back, but never getting far from the spot where he had first stopped. And all the time he looked in toward the harbor, from whence must come the rum ship. He watched it proceeding almost directly at him, and wondered if, after all, he would dare to put his plan into execution. So far it was just as he had planned, but would the rest of it work out?

Nearer and nearer approached the schooner, and Wilson sailed back and forth in front of it, as though he were just idling away the time out there in his boat. But now it was almost upon him, and old Pig Eyes was gesticulating excitedly from the bridge for him to get out of the path.

For just a moment Wilson gauged the wind. Then, with a courage worthy of a better purpose, he jerked the rudder to one side, released the boom, and leaped, with both feet, to the gunwale. The little craft jerked and ducked, and Wilson felt the water pouring over his ankles. It was done. He leaped clear of the boat, into the water. He came to the surface and grasped the overturned and sinking dory as excited shouts came from the passing schooner. What if they left him to drown? Like Pieface—those pleading eyes—

But he had judged old Pig Eyes correctly. The little man cursed profusely, but ordered his vessel brought to a stop, and sent a boat to the rescue. Wilson's heart leaped with joyful relief, and as the boat drew near he swam to meet it and was pulled aboard.

"Well, well. If it ain't the boy friend."

Wilson looked up into the face of the sailor to whom he had said good-by not two hours before.

"Yes, it's me," he said. "But I thought I was gone that time."

"What d'yer mean, boy friend?" queried the second man in the rescue boat. "D'you know the kid?"

"Sure. He's the one asked the cap to let him ship yest'day. Guess he ships now all right, all right. Hey, boy friend?"

"I guess so," said Wilson.

"Say!" The boy friend's friend suddenly looked thoughtful. "You didn' do this a purpose, did yer?"

"Try to drown hisself a purpose?" quizzed the other. "Don't be silly."

Wilson remained silent.

"No, I mean try to get rescued a purpose."

The other man looked at him, puzzled, then at Wilson, who continued his silence.

"What d'yer think he'd do that for, dumb-bell?"

"To get aboard, dumb-bell yourself; to ship, don't yer see?"

"Take a chance on drowning hisself to ship on this lousy tub? Likely. An' if he did, he'll sure get a bellyful."

"Did yer, though?" the first sailor asked Wilson, bluntly.

"Of course not," Wilson lied. "I just capsized."

"You sure did. Capsized pretty."

They pulled alongside the schooner, and Wilson scrambled up on deck, ahead of his rescuers. The skipper looked at him in surprise and evident disgust.

"You," he said.

"Yes, sir," said Wilson.

"What d'you think you were tryin' to do out there in that bo't, anyway?" barked the skipper.

"Why, I was just sailing around, and—and—it overturned."

Old Pig Eyes grunted. Then he cursed loud and fluently. Then he grunted again.

"And you," he said, at last, "you thought you was fit to be a reg'lar sailor. Ugh! You can't even sail a dory. Of all the fool stunts I ever saw, that was the foolishest that you pulled in that dory. You'd think you were trying to spill it. Say—" like the sailor, he grew suspicious as he thought of it—"were you?"

"Of course not. I merely capsized."

"Oh, you 'merely capsized,' did you." The voice was mocking. "Well, you'll wish you hadn't. That's all I got to say."

The skipper turned in his usual impatient manner and strode away. Wilson, not knowing what else to do, sat down on a bulkhead.

Well, that was that. Here he was, and he knew the skipper would not turn about now, so he was booked for the adventure. Old Pig Eyes might try to frighten him with vague threats, but he couldn't do any more than make him work, and he supposed he would have to work, anyway, if he was to make a fortune. The schooner was pushing on now, out to sea. Ahead of them only a fishing schooner was in sight; nothing else but water. What would Wembridge think now, to see his erstwhile pupil transformed into a rum-runner? What would his father think? Well, they couldn't think much worse of him than he did himself. But what could one expect of a person who would drown a dog for no reason at all? Thus he judged himself, as though he were judging a perfect stranger. But it was no stranger who was haunted by the eyes of Pieface. He arose and walked nervously about the deck.

He felt the touch of a hand on his shoulder.

"Hey, boy friend, you'd better keep your head about yer. The cap sure is plenty mad, and I don't mean maybe. He thinks you spilled a purpose."

"Thanks," said Wilson. "I'll be careful."

"It ain't no joy cruise on this tub when the cap's ugly, I'll tell yer that."

"What could he do to me?"

"What could he do to yer? Well, he could kick yer to death; or he could larrop yer to death; or he could work yer to death; or he could jes' nat'rally drop yer overboard. An' if he don't come awful near doin' one or the other, my name ain't Jack McCarthy."

After which reassuring bit of information Jack McCarthy—if his name really was that, which the police of some cities affected to doubt—strolled nonchalantly away.

Wilson gazed after him. It was no use pretending to himself that he was not frightened, because he knew he was. Yet he did not think anything very serious would come to him in the way of punishment for getting rescued. After all, if he courted the skipper's favor, everything probably would go all right. In any event, he had accomplished his aim to join the rumship crew, and if the stories he had heard were true, he might be on the way to fortune. Certainly it was better than facing Joe Kirkup again, now that Pieface was irrevocably missing.

The rum ship was drawing closer to the fishing schooner now, and Wilson walked over to the rail and looked at it, for lack of anything else to do. It was the "Alice M.," hailing from Portland, he discovered. That must be a terrible life, that fisherman life, he reflected. Fish were such smelly messy, sticky things until they had been cooked.

But why was the rum ship slowing down and pulling alongside? Old Pig Eyes was hailing the fishermen. Was the fisherman in league with the rum ship in some way? Now they were at a dead stop, and old Pip Eyes was yelling through a megaphone Wilson listened.

"Capsized in a dory—picked him up— from Miquelon—thought you might take him aboard—set him ashore sometime when you're going."

Wilson stiffened as he understood the purport of the skipper's words. They were going to send him back—back to face Joe—back where he would have to start all over again to make his fortune.

"No, no, no," he shouted, running toward the bridge. "I won't go."

But Cap'n Gus Spokes already was signifying his willingness to do as requested. And already a boat was being lowered for the transfer.

"No, no," Wilson repeated, automatically.

"So?" said old Pig Eyes, glowering down

on him. "You didn't spill her on purpose, hey? But still you don't want to go back, Hey?"

"Yes, I did," said Wilson, excitedly. "I did it on purpose. But I don't want to go back. I won't go back. I'm going to stay here."

"Git into that bo't before I throw you in," barked the skipper. "Hurry up."

He whose name might or might not have been Jack McCarthy tugged at Wilson's arm as the skipper started towards him.

"I won't," said Wilson, weakly, but he did.

Old Pig Eyes scowled at him from the deck as he clambered down into the waiting dory.

"You're lucky to get out it," said Jack McCarthy seriously, as he pulled at the oars. "The cap's a low dog."

And as if this insult to the dog kingdom had been heard and resented, there came the barking of a dog from the deck of the fishing schooner.

CHAPTER VIII

SHIPMATES

THE barking of the dog on the deck of the fisherman had sent a chill creeping up Wilson's spine. In his troubled mind now the word "dog" meant but one thing —Pieface; and though he knew that Pieface must be at the bottom of the sea, yet it also seemed that it must be Pieface that was barking from the deck of the ship.

But he could not let such muddled thoughts have control of his mind long, for Jack McCarthy already was prodding him to climb out of the dory and get aboard the schooner.

"It's a lucky break for yer, kid," said the sailor.

Wilson turned for a look at the rum ship, humoring a last hope that old Pig-Eyes might relent and call him back, but that diminutive worthy was glaring at him with a look that dissipated such an absurd hope without delay. Wilson, with unwilling feet, climbed aboard the fishing schooner, nodding a farewell to the grinning McCarthy.

He looked around at once for the dog, whose bark had been the salute that had welcomed him to the vessel, but no dog was now in sight. As a matter of fact, though Wilson had not seen the dog, the dog had seen Wilson, and his behavior had been so extraordinary that Bill Johnson had been detailed by Cap'n Gus to take him into the forecastle cabin until he should overcome his excitement.

"Guess he's been trained to distrust strangers," the cap'n had said, thus explaining to himself and to his men the dog's peculiar actions.

Cap'n Gus devoted his attention to Wilson now, as the youth confronted him.

"What happened to ye?" he inquired, bluntly.

"Boat capsized." Wilson, thoroughly unhappy at the failure of his scheme and the necessity of going back to the island, bit off the words with almost a snarl.

Cap'n Gus made the conventional clucking noise, tongue against teeth, which may express surprise, commiseration, or other feelings more handily than words. Then: "What kind of bo't?" he asked.

"Sailing dory."

Two more clucks. "Think o' that," said the cap'n. "Pretty lucky that schooner came along and rescued ye. Still luckier we happened to be here to take ye off the schooner. You prob'ly didn't know that was a rum-runner, did ye?"

"Certainly I did," Wilson snapped.

"Well, well. Guess ye must be kinder upset." The cap'n was inclined to put the kindest interpretation on Wilson's apparent ungratefulness. "Suppose ye lie down a while, and we'll do some more talking later."

"I don't want to lie down. I'm all right."

"Well, that's fine. I like to see a young feller with some spirit to him. Suppose you spin your yarn, then. Tell us who ye' are and how ye happened to get upset and all about it?"

"My name is Wilson Bersey, and— Oh, what's the use? What difference does it make to you, anyhow?"

Cap'n Gus shrugged his shoulders. The boy must be nerved up, despite his denial, he decided. The best thing was to make him feel as much at home as possible, and then let him alone for a bit.

"My name's Cap'n Gus Spokes," he said, "and you can just nose around and get acquainted with the other boys for yerself, and make yerself to home on the bo't, for I cal'late it will be a day or so before anybody will be goin' ashore."

An even darker expression came over Wilson's face at this, and the cap'n hastened to add, "Somebody'll be goin' 'fore long for sure, though, so you needn't worry but ye'll get there."

"I don't want to go back there," said Wilson.

The cap'n looked up in surprise.

"You don't?" His voice implied unbelief in what his ears had heard.

"No. I won't go back."

"What do ye want to do?"

The question was unanswerable, and Wilson glared silently at the fast-disappearing rum ship. It was now his turn to shrug

his shoulders, and he did it, signifying hopelessness.

Cap'n Gus looked at him with a measur-
ing eye. Wilson felt his gaze travel from
his head to his feet, but paid no attention.
Finally the survey was finished.

"Well," said the cap'n, "ye're a pretty
husky feller, and I cal'late I might make
some use of ye if ye wanted to try bein'
a fisherman for a while." It was evident,
the cap'n thought, that this was what the
lad had in mind. But he soon perceived his
mistake.

"A fisherman?" repeated Wilson in tones
of scorn. "I should say not."

Cap'n Gus decided that the youth was
even more upset by his experiences of the
day than even he had suspected. He didn't
want to go ashore, and he didn't want to
stay aboard. It was an *impasse*.

"Well, looks like ye'd got to bunk here
for a while, anyway," said the cap'n, good-
naturedly, "so I'll show ye where to bunk."

He walked to the forecastle, with Wilson
listlessly following. But as he opened the
hatch, the dog, which he had quite forgotten as a result of the extraordinary in-

terview with Wilson, stepped out to meet him.

"Well, old sea dog, here's—"

He stopped in wonder, as the dog drew back and crouched, tense and snarling, at his side. His white teeth glittered, as be snarled, and into his eyes had come a gleam which was far from docile. He swayed slightly on his feet, and seemed every second to grow more tense of muscle.

"What—"

The cap'n's interrogative was interrupted by a cry from the youth behind him.

"Pieface; It *is* Pieface!"

The cap'n wheeled and looked at the youth. His face had gone pale; his mouth stood agape; his head was crouched forward, and in his bulging eyes was such a look as the cap'n had not seen since his wife's aunt went crazy years ago and thought she saw a ghost.

"It can't be. It can't be. But it is," Wilson screamed.

But the cap'n had little time to find out his meaning, for now the dog leaped. With a wolf-like snarl he left the deck with all four feet, and hurled himself straight at

Wilson's throat. The youth, bending forward and totally unnerved, went over like
a tenpin as the dog's body struck him.
The dog's teeth sank in Wilson's coat collar
ripping it like so much paper.

Then, as the dog crouched for the final
spring at his fallen prey, Cap'n Gus recovered from his horrified stupor enough to
leap forward and interpose his own body.
The men came running from all parts of
the ship. Two of them yanked Wilson's
supine body to one side, while others joined
Cap'n Gus in holding back the still snarling dog. Presently, under their hands, the
dog grew calmer, and they managed to lead
him down into the forecastle cabin; but only
after he had turned several times, as though
begging for permission to finish the job
that he had started.

Inside the cabin, Bill Johnson took the
dog seriously to task.

"What kind of a way is that for a dog
to act, I ask you?" he demanded, standing
with feet wide apart in front of the offender.

The dog, though still quivering slightly
from the excitement, rubbed against the
man's leg, as a cat might do, then hopped

onto his hind legs, bracing against the man with his forepaws, and looking up at him.

"So that's it," said Bill, as though everything were explained. "Well, you see it don't happen again."

He gave the dog a reassuring pat on the head, whereupon the dog jumped back down, waiting for further instructions. Pieface knew that he had displeased his new friends by his show of rage against his erstwile new master, but he could no more have controlled himself when he saw Wilson confronting him than he could have controlled the course of the stars. Blind, unreasoning hatred, born of that moment when Wilson had left him to die in the unfriendly sea, had filled his heart and for the moment he had forgotten new friends and old friends alike, and thought only of his enemy. He did not regret his act now, but he was ready to make peace in order to keep the friendship of Cap'n Gus, Bill, and the others. That was what Bill had understood him to mean; and that was what he did mean.

Bill motioned him into a corner and left him there, bent on satisfying the curiosity

about Wilson which this unexpected encounter had aroused. But his curiosity had
to go unsatisfied for the present, for Cap'n
Gus had called Wilson into a private conference in his cabin.

Wilson, still pale and unstrung, had entered the cabin to find the cap'n no longer
the jovial, good-natured man who previously
talked with him, but stern of visage and
cold of eye. Cap'n Gus did not know what
had caused Pieface to attack the ship's guest,
but he knew that there must have been some
cause deeper than caprice. He intended to
find out what it was, and he did not expect
in the least that it would put Wilson in a
favorable light.

He was sitting at his table as Wilson was
shoved into the cabin by one of the crew,
and for a few moments he said nothing, but
stared scowlingly at his guest. Then: "Sit
down," he said.

Wilson did as ordered, and the cap'n
continued to stare. When at last he spoke,
it was with the air of a man undertaking
a painful but necessary duty.

"You know this dog," he said, as one
putting a statement, not asking a question.

Wilson nodded.

"What d'he jump ye for?"

"I don't know."

"No? We'll see about that. Whose dog is he?"

"Mine."

The cap'n expelled his breath between his teeth at this reply, as though he could not find words to express his feelings. "You must ha' been a fine master for him," he said, scornfully. "How d'ye suppose he got aboard this vessel?"

"I don't know."

"No. Well, I'll tell ye. We picked him up right out here in the water, a good four miles from shore. And what's more, I'll tell ye how I figger it out. I figger you treated that dog so mean that he jes' nat'-rally couldn't stay on the same dry land with ye any longer, and so he took to the water and swum out to us. What I want to know is, what mean trick you pulled that made him do it."

"I didn't do anything," said Wilson, nervously. "I had him out in the boat and he fell overboard; that's all."

"Why didn't ye pull him back in again?"

"I—I don't know. I—I couldn't."

"So that's it," said the cap'n, coldly, "All right, that's all."

Wilson started to leave the cabin, but the cap'n stopped him.

"Wait a minute," he said. "I kinder wish we hadn't been so ready to take a mis'rable cockroach like you aboard, but so long's you're here, I suppose we got to decide what we're goin' to do with ye."

He paused a moment, frowning in thought.

"Now in the first place," he resumed, "that dog ain't your'n no longer; he's mine. Understand that?"

Wilson nodded sullenly.

"And in the second place, so long's you don't want to go ashore, you're goin' to stay aboard. And you're goin' to earn your keep. Understand that?"

"I won't be a fisherman," declared Wilson, trying to make a show of bravery.

"Don't worry," replied Cap'n Gus. "You couldn't be a fisherman in a hundred years. You ain't constituted right. You ain't fit to associate with a good, self-respectin' fish. And besides, you don't need to worry 'bout my keeping ye on this-here schooner any longer than it'll take to finish up this little job o' fishin' and get back to Portland. My dog don't like ye—and neither do I."

He swung his chair around, turning his back on Wilson, who took this as dismissal and went out. In the forecastle cabin he could hear Pieface barking, but it was not the menacing bark of anger; rather the joyful bark of boisterous content. Wilson could tell by the commotion that Pieface was indulging his favorite pastime of pretending to be ferocious, just as he had done in the dory—to his sorrow. As he listened, he felt an unreasoning desire to enter and let Pieface finish the job that he had started an hour ago. The cap'n's biting words had only added to his own feeling of hopelessness and self-abasement. That same inexplicable urge to make himself appear heroic in his own eyes, which had prompted him to throw away his money and later to attempt to drown Pieface, now suggested this new and more dangerous gesture. He was afraid. He knew he had no desire to be chewed up by an angry dog. The mere thought of personal pain made him feel weak. Yet he felt a desire, seemingly above everything else, for the satisfaction of stepping into the cabin and facing the dog. He wanted to say: "Here I am, Pieface. Now what do you want to do to me?" And, as a matter of fact, he did not think the men in the cabin would let the dog attack him again, anyway. He was not exactly a hero.

But when he entered the cabin, he found that there was only one man there with Pieface. It was the cook. All the others had recovered sufficiently from their excitement to return to their work. The cook was playing with the dog, and had just suggested an adjournment to the galley in order that he might go to work and Pieface be refreshed, when both man and dog turned to look at the newcomer.

Wilson did not say the words that he had planned, but stood stock-still just inside the cabin. Pieface broke off a joyful bark, half uttered, and also stood stock-still. But though the cook made no move to prevent trouble, Pieface now only glared. He stiffened, ready to declare war at the first sign of an overt act, but the blind fury

which had first possessed him at the sight of
Wilson had now been tempered by his re-
gard for the others aboard the ship, who
seemed to disapprove of assault and battery,
and he was determined to let his enemy do
the attacking, if any attacking was to be
done.

The cook, eyes and mouth wide open,
watched the pantomine in silence. Thus the
three stood like statues for a space of
minutes. Finally Wilson spoke.

"Pieface," he said, with the voice of one
crying out for relief from some horrible
pain.

The dog stirred slightly, and a low growl
came from his throat, but otherwise he remained as before. But for the cook the spell
was broken.

"You'd better git out o' here," he coun-
seled.

Wilson took his advice.

CHAPTER IX

CHANGING COURSES

THE charm which Pieface seemed to have worked over the sea was short-lived. A day of successful fishing had followed his arrival aboard the "Alice M."; but one day was all. It was as though the appearance of Wilson had counteracted the dog's magical effect, and once more the dories that came alongside the schooner after the men had been pulling trawl had hardly enough fish in them to cover their bottoms.

Not in the least did this detract from the dog's popularity aboard. The day of good fishing which, as the fishermen were inclined to think, he had brought with him had only served to establish him the more securely and quickly in the rôle of ship's favorite. And although the men were prompt to give him credit for whatever bits of good luck continued to be encountered—and these were few enough now—they would not for a moment have thought of blaming him for bad luck.

And so he pattered around the deck; snoozed in the captain's cabin; strolled into the cook's galley for a quiet little snack; rode out to pull trawl with Bill Johnson or some of the others in a dory, and generally made himself as comfortable and as companionable as though he had been born and bred aboard ship.

As the dories came alongside, and the men began to toss the fish (what there were of them) into the pens on deck with forks, Pieface would stand by and watch operations with the eye of a connoisseur. To be sure, when he first witnessed this performance he had made one or two rushes toward the pens, thinking the fish were being tossed there for his amusement, and that it would be expected of him to retrieve a few of them and toss them around a bit in his jaws. But Cap'n Gus had talked to him very seriously, demonstrating his talk by holding him back with gentle but firm hands, and Pieface had understood that his task was to be that of an overseer, not a participant in the game.

Then, after the dories had all been hoisted in, came the dressing-down process, which Pieface thought the best sport of all, but which Wilson, who was undergoing a none-too-gentle tutoring at the hands of Bill Johnson in the art of being a fisherman, thought the most detestable part of his new and unwelcome occupation. Each fish had to be split, cleaned, and salted, and although Pieface revelled in the banter of the men as they went about this task, and gained a voracious appetite as he sniffed the strong odors that accompanied the operations, Wilson found it the dirtiest and messiest job he had ever encountered in his pampered existence.

When the dressing down was finished, the deck had to be scrubbed clean, and here again Pieface and Wilson reacted differently. Pieface, finding some of his human companions right down on his own level on the deck, conceived this to be a game almost equal to cleaning the fish, and he scampered joyously in the wake of this scrubber or that, circled around him and took great delight in trying to figure out in which direction the swab would go next. If he occasionally tracked up a perfectly clean spot on the deck so that it had to be scrubbed all over again, he was forgiven with remarkable good nature by most of the men.

But it was no exciting game to Wilson, who, as a matter of fact, was doing most of the scrubbing these days. Indeed, it was an altogether tiresome and hateful exercise. But in one way it was a welcome task. He had set his heart now on winning back the good graces of the dog he had used with such cowardly cruelty, and he found that he could accomplish more along that line while scrubbing the deck than at any other time. The dog so thoroughly enjoyed the sport of chasing the swab right and left and forward and back that he overlooked the fact that it was Wilson who was manipulating it. And Wilson, intent on making his peace with the dog, not only refrained from rebuking him when he tracked up a clean spot on the deck, but even encouraged him to play the swabbing game in any way he chose.

Then there was another unpleasant task which Wilson had to do, and which he used to further his suit for the dog's renewed friendliness. This was helping the cook, or, in the parlance of the fishermen, the "doctor." The doctor's galley being one of Pieface's favorite haunts, Wilson found many opportunities while at work in that portion of the ship to ingratiate himself with the dog by a friendly word or by purloining a choice morsel to toss into a corner behind the cook's back.

But he paid dearly for this privilege, for the cook, though usually as genial as he was fat,—and particularly genial to Pieface,— was a veritable slavedriver as far as his helper was concerned.

"Don't chip the skin off; scrape it off," he would shout at Wilson as the latter struggled with a seemingly bottomless bucket of potatoes, and Wilson, who had thought he was paring with great care and economy, knew better than to utter a word of self-defence. Instead, if Pieface happened to be there, the boy would look at the dog as though for sympathy, and though it was several days before the dog showed more than a studied tolerance, he presently began to succumb to Wilson's suit for forgiveness,

and accepted his advances in the same
friendly way in which he accepted those of
the other members of the crew.

Thus things went on for several days
aboard the schooner. But the fishing continued poor, and finally Cap'n Gus decided
to shift his ground. The appearance of a
large number of dogfish on the trawls was
the final straw, and one nightfall the main
trisail, under which the "Alice M." had been
jogging about, was furled, and the big mainsail was hoisted in its place. Sailing smartly
under the increased canvas, the schooner
headed out to sea.

Wilson, who had been kept unusually
busy all day, poised his weary body on the
lee rail, leaning against the foremost
shrouds, and watched the bow wave break
phosphorescent under him and spatter to
leeward as the schooner pitched easily into
the big, smooth head seas.

Pieface, having gorged himself with food,
ambled contentedly across the deck and
stretched out at his feet. It was the first
time that the dog had indicated so plainly
his altered attitude toward his would-be
murderer. Wilson withdrew his gaze from

the awesome sea, and timidly bestowed a pat on the dog's head. Pieface lay quiet under his touch, and then looked up at him, languidly content. He had not forgotten the episode of the sailing dory; it was an experience too horrible to be forgotten easily, but he had come to believe that Wilson was genuinely sorry. Indeed, in view of the marked friendship shown by the boy in the last few days, he was not at all sure that he had meant him harm. But the main factor in his change of heart was the discovery that in some inexplicable way this boy reminded him of the master whom he had loved in those earlier days when he lived on land. Something about the boy's voice when he was being kind, something about his manner when he was being playful, something about his stride when he walked across the deck—these things smacked somehow of John Bersey. And anything that smacked of John Bersey, as Pieface saw it, smacked of the divine. So he lay happily at Wilson's feet.

Wilson continued to caress the dog's head, but his eyes once again sought the phosphorescent wave as it broke endlessly against

the bow of the plowing vessel. He felt
strangely at peace with the world—a feeling
which a few days before he had thought
never to experience again. He thought of
his father's letter. "A man's dog is his best
friend." He had been angry when he read
that. Now he knew it was true. He had
regained Pieface's friendship, and now
nothing else seemed to matter. Yet—and
it was as though a sharp pain had racked
him as he thought of this—he had lost Pieface in learning the truth about him, for now
Cap'n Gus claimed him, and he had not
had the effrontery to question the claim.
Had he not deliberately abandoned the dog
to die?

Two of the fishermen strolled across the
deck.

"Thar he is," said one of them, and Wilson, thinking the men had been seeking him,
was inordinately happy. He, who had so
recently felt a consuming hate for the whole
world, suddenly discovered that he wanted
to be liked. And these men, sullen as he had
been about his work, liked him well enough
to come looking for him. So he thought.

But his mind was quickly disabused.

"Yep, thar he is," said the other of the two fishermen; "and blamed if he ain't laying right alongside the young lubber. C'm'-ere, sir, you ole sea dog." And he clapped his hands together invitingly.

Pieface rose and scampered to them, and Wilson, who had half risen when they first spoke, sank back to his seat on the rail, disappointed. But it gave his musing a new turn. Naturally Pieface would be popular aboard the ship and just as naturally he, Wilson, would be unpopular. The dog was happy, gay, companionable, while he was sullen and unsociable. Two homeless waifs, they were—he and Pieface. Both had been cast by Fate aboard this fishing vessel. But there the similarity stopped, for Pieface had fitted himself into the new life from the first, until he seemed an integral and necessary part of it; but he, Wilson, was still an outsider. And he realized now that he had made himself so. Looking into the shimmering spray that the ship was casting into the now increasing darkness, he made a great resolution. It seemed that a dog could be a teacher as well as a friend.

Next morning, shortly after daylight,

after a few preliminary soundings and a close examination of the bits of shell and weed that came up on the grease with which the bottom of the sounding lead had been armed, Cap'n Gus nodded to his crew. Without any further command they hoisted out the top dory from the nest amidship. A trawl tub, a small jug of water, and other gear were lowered to the fisherman who jumped into it, and he was left to set his trawl while the schooner got under way again. Half a mile away she dropped a second dory, and so continued until the entire sixteen, stretching out in a line eight miles long, were fishing.

Pieface watched each dory lowered, ran to the rail as the fisherman assigned to it took his place, and barked a farewell as each was left behind. Wilson, meantime, seemed to be taking more interest than formerly, and stepped briskly about any task in which there seemed to be occasion for his services. So much interest did he show that Bill Johnson, who was one of the last to be left behind, took it upon himself to explain various things about fishing which he had considered

it a waste of breath to explain while his pupil
was in his previous mood.

"We fish two men to a dory in the winter,"
he said, as one of the dories was being
lowered, "but one's enough in this weather."

After the last dory had been dropped,
Cap'n Gus put the schooner about and
cruised back along the line of dories, while
the cook and an ancient mariner known as
Old Ike, who was too old for dory work,
furled the jib and mainsail and reset the
main trisail. Wilson, acting on his new
resolution, helped as much as he could, and
the men were surprised at the amount of help
he was able to render them. Pieface, finding
every one too busy to play with him, snoozed
in the captain's cabin.

As the schooner slid past to leeward of
the first few dories that had been dropped,
the men already were pulling their trawls,
and Cap'n Gus smiled as he saw that nearly
every hook bore a shimmering fish—mostly
cod, with a sprinking of haddock and a few
halibut.

"Struck fish this time, by gum," he informed the cook as the latter came on deck

for a breath of air. "Look thar, now, Jim's got a whale."

"Hoy, Pat," he hailed later, as the "Alice M." rounded to leeward of the last dory. "Gettin' a catch?"

"Goin' to fill the dory, skipper," came the hearty response. The skipper squinted happily back at the fisherman.

With her jumbo backed to windward and her helm hard down, the schooner lay to for a few minutes until the fisherman, Pat, with an upraised oar, signified that he had finished pulling. A few minutes later he was forking fish over the rail, his dory sunk nearly to her gunwales with the weight of them. When they were all in the kids, Pat climbed aboard, snatched a mug-up and a bit to eat in the galley, dropped a tub of bait into his dory, and went back to make another set, while the schooner jogged up to the next dory.

It was dark that night when the last dory was hoisted aboard, and then the day's work was far from done, for there remained a large part of the catch still on deck. Hours later they were all salted down in the hold, and the crew tumbled into their bunks. most of them not even troubling to remove their rubber boots. A deck watch of one man was maintained, however, each watch being relieved by a fresh man after an hour of duty, and before daylight the man on watch called the rest of the crew. The cook had a huge breakfast ready, and in the first gray light of dawn the dories went out again. It was just such another day as that preceding it.

The third day dawned late, under a sullen bank of low-hanging cloud, beneath which a southeast wind, not yet heavy, muttered threateningly. After the first set, the dories were hoisted in and left on deck. The last few were brought alongside in a sea which threatened to crush them against the schooner's side, and the two nests of dories amidship were secured with extra lashings. The sea was getting up, and the wind had "a heft to it," as Cap'n Gus remarked. Before the cleaning was finished, a comber climbed aboard over the "Alice M.'s" weather bow and put an end to the work by washing a few tons of fish over the lee rail.

Cap'n Gus cursed briefly, cast a critical

eye over the schooner's gear, and went below.

For three days there was no fishing. These were great days for Pieface. In cabin and forecastle the men smoked, slept, played cards and spun yarns, but the dog was the favorite diversion, and he enjoyed life so thoroughly that he would have been willing to have the storm last indefinitely.

For Wilson, too, the storm served a purpose. While it did not give him a chance to show his zest for work, which was part of his resolution, it did give him a chance to make himself more agreeable with the men, which was the other part of his resolution. And thus following the dog's example, he found himself becoming more a part of the ship community. Life became increasingly pleasant.

He sat chatting with Bill Johnson on the third day of inactivity, while Pieface, who had become more and more friendly, lay at his feet.

"Isn't this an awful storm?" he said to Bill, as the crash of the sea breaking against the schooner's bow made her tremble.

"Storm!" Bill snorted. "Why this ain't

no storm. Jest a leetle too rugged to fish; that's all. If we had a full fare we'd be reaching for Portland with every rag on her. We got plenty o' sea room here— nothin' to leeward for us to bump except more water, so we sit here comfortable and rests up against it clears. The more rain, the more rest, as the feller says. You ain't seen nothin' yet, boy. Why the 'Alice' is only two thirds loaded, and she's ridin' like a tight kag."

"Ruther she'd blow a little than thicken up," some one croaked from a berth. "Thick weather's when we catch it. We ain't had much this trip, but most gen'rally there's plenty o' fog. They make it up here on these banks."

"Shut up," came the shout from another bunk. "You want to call a fog on us with yer talk?"

"Fog," mused Wilson, his hand playing idly over Pieface's head. "I think I've been in a sort of fog myself."

Bill Johnson seemed to understand, and smiled. "Hope you come out of the next one you get in as well," he said, softly.

CHAPTER X

FOG

O N the morning of the fourth day of the
storm the wind had dropped. The sea
still looked far too heavy for comfort to
Wilson's inexperienced eyes, but he was
determined to overcome his well-deserved
unpopularity aboard, and therefore he did
all he could to help as the dories were
launched, and kept his opinions to himself.
By afternoon the sun was out, and only the
extra-high rollers bore witness to the fact
that there had been a blow.

Wilson, mindful of his resolution, went
about his tasks all day with a new cheerful-
ness. The cook and Old Ike noticed it, and
were correspondingly pleasant. Cap'n Gus
noticed it, too, but was still inclined to be
gruff. He looked with some suspicion on
this radical change of disposition, and
several times called Pieface away when the
dog, now completely reconciled, trotted in

Wilson's wake from place to place about the ship. But Wilson, when the skipper was not looking, would signal to the dog and the latter would trot confidently back to him again. Finally Cap'n Gus gave up trying to keep them separated, partly because he trusted Pieface's ability to take care of himself in case of trouble, and partly because he was inclined to trust the dog's intuition as to the sincerity of Wilson's friendship.

Next morning Wilson decided on a new step towards making himself a fisherman. He approached Bill Johnson as the latter was getting ready to start his day's fishing.

"May I go in the dory with you?" he asked.

"Suits me," said Bill, looking at him approvingly. "Better speak to the skipper about it, though."

Wilson did as Bill suggested, and Cap'n Gus nodded his consent. It had occurred to the skipper that with Wilson out in a dory, he would not have to worry about a set-to with Pieface.

But the skipper had made a miscalculation, for as Wilson and Bill puttered around getting things ready for their descent into the dory, Pieface puttered with them. Bill, letting Wilson assemble most of the fishing gear, rolled him over, played with him and shouted at him, to the dog's infinite delight. Finally he suggested, "Let's take the pup along, too, hey?"

"Yes, let's," replied Wilson, who had been trying to summon up courage to make the suggestion himself.

Their dory was launched, and when it was overboard the schooner came about and left them. The skipper, being busy elsewhere, did not see them take Pieface aboard, thereby upsetting his plan to keep the dog and his former master separated. The dog made himself comfortable in the bow, and Bill turned his attention to the business of fishing.

Wilson was more or less accustomed to small boats, but as the schooner stood away he had a sudden feeling that a twenty-foot dory a hundred or more miles from land is a lonesome spot. Bill was so matter-of-fact, however, and Pieface so completely at ease, that he shook off the feelings.

"Can't I help you set the trawl, Bill?" he asked.

Bill shook his head. "Later you work, son," he said.

He dropped the killick, a primitive sort of anchor to hold the trawl, then started paying out the quarter mile of heavy line from which dangled the shorter lines with the hooks at their ends. Last of all came the trawl buoy, a small black keg, and to this Bill fastened the boat's short painter.

"Now we sit and I smoke for a couple hours," he said, and then we start to pull.

The schooner was by this time hull down to the northwest, and the nearest dory visible was only a speck occasionally tossed up on the crest of the sea. One minute their own dory was on the crest, and the skyline was many miles away. The next minute it had slid into the trough, and lay at the bottom of a valley of water perhaps twenty feet deep and two hundred feet wide.

Pieface, enjoying this novel experience barked vigorously every time the dory sank into the trough. As they rode the crest again, he panted with excitement, waiting for the inevitable drop. It was a new game, and a joyous one.

Bill laughed at him. Then, noticing that

Wilson seemed to be taking things more seriously than Pieface, he said, "The Atlantic Ocean's a large place, son, but when ye get used to it, like we are, it don't seem so big, long's ye got a good stout boat under ye."

Wilson looked at the blue water as it rolled past, a scant two feet below the gunwale of the dory.

"It's not only large, this ocean," he observed, "but it seems to me it's very, very wet."

Bill grinned. "You'll do," he grunted.

Pieface grew weary of his sport, and made his way gingerly back to Wilson, settling down comfortably at his feet　Wilson stroked his head, musing. The schooner, by now, would be nearly back to the other end of the string of dories. Their dory had been the last one launched.

A comber passed under it, and Wilson saw Bill look into the southwest. He heard a soft oath muttered by the fisherman. Wondering, he followed his tutor's glance, and saw on the skyline what looked like a low bank of cloud.

"Fog," Bill explained, briefly.

"Oh," said Wilson.

Then, after a pause: "How will the schooner find us if it shuts down on us?"

"Well, of course she'll start from the first dory," said Bill, "and she knows the direction, 'cause she lays all her dories down on one course, and so she just sails back along the line and picks us all up."

"Oh," said Wilson again, somewhat ashamed of the fears he had implied in his question.

But presently they crowded back upon him, and another question came unbidden from his mouth: "Don't they ever miss a dory?"

"Sometimes," grunted Bill, curtly.

The fisherman bit the corner off a plug of black tobacco, and stepped over the reclining Pieface into the bow of the dory.

"Now you take them oars and keep her comin' ahead easy, just so's to take the pull off the trawl," he instructed.

He seemed to have put all thought of the fog bank out of his mind, but Wilson, as he stood up, looked at it again. It seemed appreciably nearer and higher already. He looked to leeward for the schooner, but could

not see her nor anything else on the face of
the waters except the hump of a finback
whale cruising lazily past them. Bill went
methodically about his work. Pieface, dozing, snored peacefully. Wilson gritted his
teeth and fought to keep his nerve.

The youth was accustomed now to the
quick motion of the dory in the seaway, and
he balanced on his feet in the narrow bottom,
facing forward as he had seen the fishermen
do. Thus he shoved the dory forward with
short strokes, while Bill pulled the trawl in
over the bow, slatted each fish off the hook
with a practised flip, and coiled the line
neatly in its tub. Occasionally an obstreper-
ous fish was whacked over the head with the
gob stick before being tossed into the pen,
which was formed in the midship two-thirds
of the dory by movable boards. A halibut
or an especially big cod had to be landed
with the gaff hook, lest its weight break the
line or straighten out the hook in its mouth
when it was hauled out of the water.

Once or twice Bill straightened his back
and glanced to windward, where the fog
bank was drifting down on them before the
southwester. By the time they were halfway

up the trawl the bank was very close. Bill gazed at it a minute, then turned and looked in the direction in which the "Alice M." lay. As a great wave tossed them skyward, they caught a glimpse of her sails. Wilson could see that the mainsail had been hoisted in place of the trisail, indicating that they were hurrying to get all the dories aboard as quickly as possible.

Suddenly a damp breath seemed to blow across the dory, chilling its occupants to the bone. A minute later and sea and sky alike were blotted out in a fleecy whiteness. It was as though this vague, monotonous whiteness bore down on them with actual weight. Space did not exist—only this oppressive white weight, which held them like a vice.

Bill bit off a fresh quid of tobacco and continued silently to pull trawl. Pieface, awakened by the damp breath that had chilled him, stood up and looked about him for a moment in wonder, then turned his gaze to the fish that flopped in the pen, and barked at them fiercely. Wilson tried to gulp down the lump in his throat, and said nothing.

The trawl was nearly in, and the dory more than half full of fish. Bill heaved in on the trawl, as an unusually steep sea reared under them. The dory suddenly seemed to lose its tension, and Bill stumbled backward with the line slack in his hand. The bow was tossed high on the crest of the wave.

"Blarsted rotten trawl line," muttered Bill, and a frown settled over his face. The dory spun around, and Wilson lost all sense of direction.

"Gimme them oars," said Bill, settling on a bow thwart. Wilson obeyed silently. Bill pulled a little, holding the head of the dory to wind and sea, and sat silent. He was trying to hold the dory, as near as he could guess, where it had been when the line broke.

But the banks are a place of cross currents. For an hour they sat there. Then, faintly, the dismal moan of the schooner's foghorn came to them. It might have been ahead, astern, abeam. It simply echoed softly out of the uncanny fog.

"Beller," Bill ordered, and rising to his feet he roarded a wordless hail into the dense, limitless whiteness. Wilson added his shout, and Pieface, catching the spirit, howled long and loud. Then they listened. For a half a minute they heard only each other's heavy breathing. Then came the sound of the schooner's horn again, but still seeming to come from nowhere in particular.

Half an hour of intermittent shouting brought them nothing but hoarse throats. The schooner's horn became more and more indistinct. Finally they heard it no more.

"Missed us," commented Bill, unemotionally.

Pieface, not quite sure what it was all about, continued to howl and bark from time to time. Bill reached down and patted him.

"No use to beller any more, Pieface," he said.

Wilson tried to appear as calm as his dorymate. "What do we do now?" he asked.

"We go for a row," said Bill. "Like rowin', son?"

"Sure," said Wilson.

Bill looked at him with mild approbation. "Well, you'll get some," he said. "We're rowin' for Miquelon unless we get picked up meantime, which ain't improbable."

"Have you a compass?"

"Nope. Lay a course by the wind and sea. Keep 'em 'bout four points on the port bow and we hit Miquelon some time or other if the wind don't shift."

Bill settled down to an easy, unhurried stroke. Wilson slipped the extra pair of oars into the tholepins.

"You fork most o' them fish overboard before you start to row, boy," directed Bill. "This-here packet ain't carryin' no excess cargo. Leave a few in the bottom, though. Might want 'em."

CHAPTER XI

ON THE HIGH SEA

TWO men and a dog in a dory a hundred miles or more from land. Irretrievably lost from their ship. Enveloped in fog. No compass. No provisions. Yet Bill Johnson rowed calmly, as though it were all in the day's work. His young helper, having cast most of the day's catch overboard, as instructed, took up the other pair of oars and rowed silently, though his heart pounded. Pieface was instinctively aware that all was not well, but not knowing just what the danger was, he disregarded it and took his favorite position in the bow, barking companionably from time to time.

"Did you ever get lost like this before?" asked Wilson, trying hard to keep his voice from betraying the panic within him.

"Three winters ago," said Bill, in a conversational tone, "I was adrift four days. Cold weather then. This ain't half bad.

Feller with me that trip lost some fingers and toes. Frostbite. This-here's yachting weather."

Bill, knowing the ocean, had misgivings in his heart, but he let no trace of them creep into his voice.

They rowed on as dismal hour followed dismal hour. The fog weighed down on them with its terrible monotony, and seemed to rob them of all progress. Pieface dropped off to sleep several times, always awakening to start a fresh serenade of barking. He sensed the low spirits of his companions, and felt it encumbent upon himself to encourage them as much as possible. He succeeded so well that every time his serenade started, the dory seemed to push more hardily through the fog, and conversation would begin anew between the two rowers.

It was in the midst of one of these conversational outbreaks in mid-afternoon that Wilson summoned up courage to speak of something that had been in his mind for hours.

"I'm thirsty," he ventured.

"So'm I," said Bill, shortly, and Wilson understood that the subject was, for the present, taboo. He continued to row, and the thirst grew greater and greater as he thought about it. And he could not turn his mind away from it. There was a gallon jug in the bow. The water must be cool and sweet, he thought.

An hour later he tried again. "When do we get a drink?"

"Come night."

Picface, standing in the bow with open mouth, gave Wilson an idea. He tried to suck the thick fog into his parched mouth, as the dog seemed to be doing, and it helped a little. But the steady creak, creak of the oars on the tholepins was getting on his nerves.

It was always Pieface that renewed his resolution. Something in their past relationship was constantly recurring to him, always with the effect of making Pieface seem his reason for living and striving. From being a symbol of all that made life miserable, the dog had become a symbol of all that is worth while in life, and his very bark struck new courage into the youth's heart, new strength into his tired arms. He did not try to understand why. He just vaguely realized that this was true.

And now, as Pieface uttered a cheerful yelp, he held his ragged nerves in check, and restrained himself from making a dive for the water jug or doing some other rash thing—he hardly knew what.

Sometimes the fog seemed to thin out a little, and they could see a hundred yards ahead, or, perhaps, two hundred yards. At other times it was so thick about them that it actually seemed to hold the dory in check as it butted into the dense bank. The hands of the rowers were blistered— particularly Wilson's. The cotton gloves they wore only lessened the friction, without eliminating it.

The dismal hours dragged on, and suddenly it was night. With the quick darkening of the sky came a drop in temperature, but neither of the rowers felt cold. The sudden blast of cold which had preceded the fog had been only a passing phenomenon, and though the fog itself was far from warm, the exercise of rowing had been sufficiently heat-producing.

Now Bill spoke welcome words. "Let's have a drink o' water."

But also a warning: "Just a mouthful now, mind. That gallon's got to last us."

Wilson obeyed, and passed the jug back. Pieface, who had retreated to the stern sheets, had been licking the dampness from the sides of the dory, and Bill, noticing this, conserved the dog's share.

Hunger, as well as thirst, was making itself known in the boat. Pieface announced his feelings in a little whine, but when Bill and Wilson both talked to him, he understood from the voices that they realized his hunger and sympathized with him, but were unable to satisfy it. He became quiet. The men, too, were hungry, but no word of it was spoken.

"Tired, kid?" asked the fisherman, as the darkness settled down.

"A little."

"Well, curl up aft there and get yourself some sleep. "I'll row alone for a while."

Wilson shipped his oars, and made his way to the after end of the dory, where Pieface already was snoring and whining hungrily in his sleep. The youth lifted the dog up, curled up in the narrow stern, and then laid Pieface down beside him. Pieface stretched himself, as he was thus aroused from his sleep, walked forward and then aft again, and settled down in the hollow of Wilson's side. But Wilson did not know it. He was sound asleep before the dog's short promenade had ended.

Sometime in the night he awoke suddenly. He had been dreaming that he was tied hand and foot on an iceberg, and that a polar bear was roaring at him. As his eyes opened the polar bear materialized into Pieface, and instead of rushing at him he was merely standing and looking. But the roar was repeated. It did not come from Pieface, but from somewhere without the dory.

"Steamer about somewhere," said Bill's voice from the gloom forward. He had stopped rowing.

Sixty seconds, and again came the roar from the fog. It was no schooner's foot-operated tooter, but the howl of a steam whistle.

"Big liner, comin' fast," said Bill.

"She'll pick us up?" Wilson asked ex

citedly. He was shivering with cold and dampness, and every muscle ached, but he scrambled to his feet.

"Maybe," said Bill, doubtfully.

Again the roar, seemingly overhead, and as it died out Bill shouted. A sound as of waterfall was coming from near at hand. It seemed to drown out the man's voice. Dimly through the fog Wilson glimpsed the glow of lights, almost alongside, and he screamed his loudest. Pieface joined his mightiest howl to the general clamor.

The wash from the bow of the liner picked the dory up and tossed her sidewise. The whistle sounded again, already further away. Wilson screamed again, with real terror in his voice, and Pieface, alarmed at the tone of the scream, barked angrily at the darkness.

"No use yellin', kid," said Bill, at length keeping his own voice steady only by great effort. "They couldn't see us, nor they couldn't hear us over all their own noises."

Wilson, stunned, sat silent, fighting his terror. Alone, he was sure he would have gone mad, but the presence of Pieface, still barking as though to frighten away whatever was threatening, together with the coolness of the fisherman, now rowing patiently again, steadied him, and he curled up again in the stern. But sleep refused to return.

"I'll row a while," he said, at last.

Bill grunted assent, and he took up his oars. Pieface went back to sleep, though with less comfort, now that he had been deprived of his pillow.

After daylight Bill portioned out another small drink from the water jug.

"What wouldn't I give for something to eat," Wilson mourned.

Bill looked at him speculatively, almost humorously. "We have food," he said.

"What?" Wilson looked quickly around the dory. Then, remembering stories he had read of men adrift on the ocean, he shuddered, partly from horror, partly from anger at the thing he believed the fisherman was suggesting.

"If you mean Pieface," he half screamed, "you can eat me first."

"No, no, no," said Bill quickly, soothingly. "Don't be gettin' such fool thoughts into your head. I mean them fish."

"Oh!" Wilson breathed a deep sigh. "So that was why you had me leave some of them. I had forgotten." He grinned sheepishly.

Still the thought of eating fresh fish did not appeal, and his appetite seemed to lose its edge. Pieface, now whining again as his hunger tortured him, was not so particular, and when Bill cut off a strip of cod and tossed it to him, he gobbled it gladly, if not with relish.

Daylight had shown the rowers nothing new. The fleecy wall of fog still pressed in from every direction, stifling; the oily, heaving, gray sea tossed the dory on its surface.

"Think you could keep this boat headed about the way she is while I catch forty winks," Bill asked.

Wilson nodded.

"Just keep the sea broad on your port bow," Bill directed, and lay down in the bow.

Like Wilson, he dropped off to sleep in the space of a few seconds. Wilson noted

that he slept on the water jug, and smiled
at the precaution.

Pieface sat quietly in the stern and
watched Wilson while he rowed. From time
to time Wilson rested on his oars, and
talked to the dog in a low voice. Pieface
pricked up his ears attentively, sometimes
replying in short, sharp barks. The voice
of the boy was so like John Bersey's voice;
and the boy, too, had grown to be like
John Bersey in other ways lately. Sometimes he wondered if this could be the
same boy who left him out there in the sea.

It was perhaps two hours after Wilson
had assumed control of the dory—though
it seemed like two weeks—that he noticed
Pieface suddenly sitting attentively erect
and straining his ears. He had not been
talking for a half hour, and Pieface had
been sitting quietly in his place. He paused
in his stroke, and straightened his back.

He strained his own ears, wondering
what Pieface was hearing, but no sound
came to them. Still he rested on his oars.
His hands were raw, sticking to the cotton
gloves with their own blood. His back
seemed well-nigh broken. His arms were

like lead. His stomach was very empty, and his mouth parched and of unclean taste. Was it any use to keep on rowing, with the slim chance of making Miquelon? Was not their only chance that of being picked up by a passing vessel, and was not that chance just as good if they drifted with the tide? He looked at Pieface. No, he must row on.

But again, as he rowed, Pieface pricked up his ears. Then, as though he had confirmed an impression of which he was not sure, he looked at Wilson and barked eagerly. Again the rower paused in his stroke, and listened. And this time he heard a faint rumble across the water to windward. He looked at the sleeping fisherman, whose ears had become so attuned to Pieface's barking that he slept on in spite of it. Then he listened again. A space of two minutes or more passed, during which he barely kept the boat's head to sea, and no sound came. Then the rumble again, scarcely louder than before.

"Bill," he called. He had meant to speak softly, but his voice came with a shout that brought the fisherman to his feet. "There's another steamer around."

Pieface was barking excitedly, but at a sign from Bill he stopped, and the older man stood rigid, listening. Again came the rumble, still far away. But minute by minute it grew more distinct. As though by way of good omen, the fog seemed to be getting a little lighter.

"She's takin' her time, whatever she is," Bill commented. "Must be a small steamer."

A half hour passed, while the sound of the foghorn grew steadily louder and more distinct. Soon they could hear a vague c-chug, c-chug, c-chug as of a steam engine.

"She's goin' to pass middlin' close by us," said Bill, a note of hope creeping into his voice. "Maybe we don't have to eat them raw codfish after all."

The next blare of the horn was closer.

"Let's give her a blast," said Bill, and together they roared. Pieface started anew his shrill barking, judging the ban to be off.

Hardly had the sounds left their throats when a dark blot in the fog took shape, and a small steamer appeared not a hundred yards away. They roared louder, and

Pieface's yelping increased proportionately in volume. The bow of the steamer swung towards them, and they saw two men leaning out of the pilot-house windows, while, another on the forecastle head shouted and pointed to them.

Methodically Bill Johnson picked up his oars and swung the dory in under the steamer's low midship rail to leeward. Some men on deck dropped a pilot ladder overside.

Wilson hugged Pieface to him. "We're saved," he shouted.

Pieface wagged his tail and surveyed the side of the steamer inquisitively.

CHAPTER XII

S ORRY to intrude, sir," said Bill Johnson, grinning, "but we was gettin' a
mite lonesome out here in the ocean—not
to say hungry."

The captain of the steamer, a big, fair-
haired, square-jawed, red-faced man,
grinned in reply. "Well, well," he said.
"It's all right. We'll keep you company
and feed you, too." There was just the
trace of a foreign accent in his speech.

"You've not been adrift long," he continued. It was a statement rather than a
question, for his new guests, though fa-
tigued, were still far from exhausted.

"Jest last night," Bill confirmed.

The captain nodded, and motioned for
them to follow him below, where he super-
intended operations while the cook placed
food and water before Bill and Wilson on
the table, and before Pieface on the floor.

Both men and dog satisfied their thirst first, and then ate ravenously. The captain sat patiently still, waiting for them to finish before asking explanations.

Pieface was the first to end the meal. He licked his chops, sighed luxuriously, and gave his attention to his new surroundings. The captain made an inviting gesture with his hands, and Pieface strolled leisurely in his direction. He was becoming accustomed to sudden changes now, and was quite prepared to make himself comfortable on this ship, as he had on the last. He had been as thoroughly dissatisfied with the cramped little dory as had his companions, and it was a distinct relief to be aboard a ship again, with a stomach full of food. In this mood he approached the captain, and readily submitted to his friendly overtures.

Presently Wilson leaned back in his chair and uttered a grunt of satisfaction, whereupon Pieface turned away from the captain and went to the youth's side. Wilson let a languid hand rest on the dog's head, and both seemed perfectly content with life at the moment.

"That's the best meal I ever ate," said

Wilson; and Bill, swallowing a final gulp of hot coffee, grinned from behind his cup.

"That's a good dog," said the captain, by way of opening the conversation.

"That-there's a real sea dog, sir," said Bill. "Name's Pieface."

Then, knowing the captain was waiting for it, Bill briefly sketched the episode that had brought them to their present situation. He mentioned only the most salient facts, except when he elaborated on the courage of his young companion or the unruffled disposition of the dog. The latter already was snoozing happily.

"Yes, yes," said the captain, when Bill had finished. "Well, my name is Carlson, and this is the steamer 'Sturdy,' bound for Hudson Bay with supplies for trading posts. We expect to be gone all summer, but if you can put up with that, I think we can find enough for you two to keep you busy until we get back."

"Cap'n Carlson," said Bill, "we're that downright grateful to ye for pickin' us up, I swear 'twouldn't make any difference if ye was to be gone five years in Hudson Bay. Not after that meal." And he patted his stomach appreciatively. "What do you say, Wilt?"

It was the first time the fisherman had addressed Wilson thus familiarly and affectionately, and his feeling of satisfaction with the world became even more profound. "Suits me," he said.

"You'd better turn in and get some sleep now," said the captain. "I see that—what do you call him?—Pieface—he's beatin' you to it."

"Oh, say, Captain," said Wilson, "you don't mind having Pieface along too, do you? I'll try to earn his keep."

"Well, now," Captain Carlson replied, giving Bill a sly and playful wink, "I don't know about that. You see we've got to think about our provisions on a long voyage like this, and I doubt if you can much more than earn your own keep."

"Oh, yes, I can. And Bill will do more than his share, too. Besides, what could you do with him if you didn't take him along?"

"Well, now, we might just drop him overboard some dark night."

Wilson instinctively grabbed the dog with

such a force that Pieface awoke with a bark of surprise. "Oh, no, no. You can't do that."

"There, there, my youngster," said the captain, "I did not think you would take me so seriously. Of course we will keep your Pieface with us. Did not Bill say he was a real sea dog? Yes, yes."

Wilson felt rather foolish for displaying his emotion before these two men, and his embarrassment became more acute when Pieface, not in the least understanding the motive that had led to his rude awakening in the midst of a very pleasant dream, withdrew himself and stalked in dignified displeasure to an opposite corner. There he went back to sleep promptly, and substituted a new dream for the one which had been interrupted.

In a few minutes Wilson and Bill were crawling into the bunks that had been prepared for them, and the captain had left them.

"Well, Wilt, here we are, as the feller says," remarked Bill.

"The others will think we're drowned," said Wilson.

"If they do, we'll fool 'em. This looks like a real pleasant cruise, if ye should ask me."

"Yes. Captain Carlson is nice, too, isn't he?"

"Real nice feller, to be sure. Square-head."

"Do you mean he's Swedish."

"Sounds like it. Somethin' like that."

"I like him."

Bill's reply was a snore. And without further ado Wilson settled down in his bunk and went to sleep. Somewhere Pieface also was sleeping. All northward bound.

Pieface was the first of the trio to awake next day. He had slept more in the dory than his two human companions, and though the comfort of the ship insured a more pleasant bed than had been available in the smaller craft, yet he had been aroused by the first sounds on shipboard after daybreak, and started a tour of inspection.

He was very much pleased with the steamer, for although it lacked many of the intriguing features of the fishing schooner, it was larger and had more nooks and corners to be explored. Its movement in the swell of the sea was not so pronounced, either, and he could run here and there with less danger of losing his temper by a sudden lurch which would upset his sense of direction. On the schooner he had managed to conceal these moments of anger, but they had galled him. It was a relief to feel himself the master of his own movements again.

In various parts of the ship he came upon strange men, some of whom called to him or reached out to pat him as he passed by. He met them all with calm equanimity, but his spirit this morning was too lofty to allow him to become playful. This big ship (as it seemed to him), the tang of salt air in his nostrils, the invigorating breeze that ruffled his light coat; all these worked together to inspire in Pieface a sense of sublime happiness. No longer was he the clownish little pup that had attracted the sympathetic affection of John Bersey. He was Pieface, the sea dog.

"Well, well, it is my friend Pieface."

The object of the remark turned and looked up into the face of Captain Carlson.

"Why do they call you Pieface?" continued the captain. And, indeed, the name that had so well fitted the pup was a gross libel on the appearance of the bright-eyed dog that now stood before him. But Pieface had no way of knowing that his name did not do him justice. He knew it only as his name. If he had given the matter any thought at all, doubtless he would have thought that it must be a good name, else how could its bearer be so content as he was this morning.

The captain continued to talk, and Pieface, recognizing the superiority of this man and understanding that he was a friend, gazed steadfastly at him as he talked and responded at intervals with a friendly bark. When the captain finally stopped talking, Pieface took up the burden of the conversation, and uttered a long series of loud barks.

"All right," the captain laughed, "if you feel that way about it we will go see how your friends are this morning. They must be awake after that outburst of noise."

He was so far right that as they went below towards the quarters where Bill and Wilson had slept, they met Bill.

"Mornin', Cap'n," he said. "Ready to go to work."

"You get your breakfast first, and then we'll see about work," replied the captain. "Is the boy up?"

"Jest openin' one eye when I left him."

"Well, Pieface and I will see if he has the other one open. The cook is waiting breakfast for you."

"That sure is service for shipboard," grinned Bill, as he strode breakfastward.

They found Wilson with one leg in his trousers. He looked up, startled, as he saw the captain. Perhaps he had overslept on his first day as a member of the steamer's crew. The captain's face, quite without expression, neither confirmed nor dissipated his misgivings. When at last the captain spoke, however, his voice was reassuring.

"Good morning, Wilson," he said.

"Good morning, sir. I hope I'm not late."

"Well, Pieface was up a little before you, but I guess if you hurry there will still be some breakfast left. How do you feel this morning?"

"Oh, fine, thank you sir." Wilson was determined to make a better start with this captain than he had with Cap'n Gus, and chose his words and tone carefully before speaking. He hurriedly adjusted his clothing and strode away to join Bill. Pieface who had been standing beside the captain turned and trotted after him.

The captain, gazing after them, wagged his head, and the corners of his lips seemed to twitch upwards. Something seemed to have pleased him.

The cook, a little Greek called Tony, greeted Wilson and Pieface cheerfully, considering the fact that breakfast should have been over a half hour before they arrived in his sanctum.

"You fill pretty good this morning, eh?" he challenged. "I make you fill better." And to carry out his promise he placed a great bowl of porridge before Wilson, and, grimacing merrily, lured Pieface into a corner where he placed a tempting dish of odds and ends, especially prepared for what Tony believed to be the most exacting canine taste.

Breakfast over, Bill and Wilson went to report to the captain. As they walked, Bill talked.

"Comfortable little tub," he said, "but kinder old and leaky, I should say. Not but what I'm glad enough to be on her, mind, and I don't doubt she'll weather the voyage and many another. These small steamers seem to hang on indefinite sometimes."

"Well, it's not a floating palace, and that is a fact," Wilson agreed, "but it certainly beats rowing all over the ocean in a dory."

"Sure does. And what's more, that Cap'n Carlson is one white feller. Did ye see how he took to Pieface right first off. Talks sort of educated like, too."

"There he is now," said Wilson. They approached the captain.

"Had breakfast?" the captain asked.

"Plenty," said Bill, and Wilson nodded agreement.

"Well, I suppose it's up to me now to find something for you to do," said the captain. "Of course there won't be a great deal of work while we're at sea. Heaviest part of your job will be when we begin hitting the trading posts. Still I guess we can find enough to keep you from getting bored with life on shipboard. I'll speak to the mate about it by and by."

He paused as Pieface came trotting up, and clapped his hands together. Pieface looked at Wilson and Bill, and seeing no objections registered accepted the invitation to frolic with the captain. The latter, laughing happily, pushed the dog playfully, jumped backward, then forward again, and again pushed, setting Pieface into a furiously happy burst of barking. Wilson and Bill joined in the captain's laughter.

"Guess I won't have him thrown overboard after all," said the captain to Wilson.

Wilson grinned sheepishly.

"You take him now," the captain continued, and go find Mr. Peters, the mate, and tell him I sent you. Perhaps he will put you to work."

Wilson turned obediently and signed to Pieface to follow. Bill took an uncertain step in the same direction, not quite sure whether the command included him.

"No, Bill," said the captain. "I want to talk with you a bit."

After Wilson and Pieface were out of earshot, he said: "That's a great dog, Bill, and I rather think the boy is the right stuff too. Tell me about them."

Bill told all he knew, which was still far from the whole story, for Wilson had kept silent about his past life, from sulkiness at first; afterwards, from fear of appearing boastful. Thus Bill's story went only back as far as Pieface's appearance in the water off Miquelon and Wilson's subsequent appearance on the rum-runner.

"What did you say the lad's name is?" asked the captain.

"Bersey," said Bill. "Wilson Bersey."

"H'm," said the captain. "That's a strange story, Bill. Bersey, eh? I wonder—"

"What did you say?" asked Bill, thinking he had lost some of the captain's words.

"Nothing, Bill, nothing. I was just mumbling to myself—and thinking. You like dogs, Bill?"

"Oh, sure."

"Well, I'll tell you that Pieface is a good one."

They walked together across the deck. "Oh, Peters," Captain Carlson hailed.

"Yay-uh?" was the reply.

"Peters, this is Bill Johnson, the fisherman we picked up yesterday. Peters is my mate, Bill."

The men shook hands.

"You take Bill in tow for a while, will you Peters?" the captain continued. "And, by the way, did you find something for the boy to do?"

"Yay-uh."

"Fine," said the captain.

As he walked away, the captain was again mumbling to himself. "Bersey," he muttered. "I wonder—"

CHAPTER XIII

PLUGUGLY

MR. Peters, the mate, was more generally and familiarly known as Plugugly. He might have acquired the name
either because of his appearance or because
of his disposition. It fitted him well in
either case. He was a man larger than the
average, but his bulk was of that unimpressive sort that seemed to have been fostered
by free play of the appetites rather than
by the development of physique. Yet a
mashed-in nose and cauliflower ears bore
witness to the fact that at some time of
his life he must have been sufficiently sound
of body to participate in some rather vigor-
ous encounters in the boxing arena; and
even now, at middle age, the appearances
of flabbiness was somewhat deceptive, as
more than one sailor had found out to his
sorrow.

Plugugly was the ship's disciplinarian,

and he enjoyed the rôle. Captain Carlson's word, of course, was law, and there never was any question of disobedience when that word came from his lips. The captain understood this, and never doubted that his commands would be followed out. But Plugugly Peters was of a different school. He worked on the theory that no command would be obeyed unless it were given in a fierce tone and enforced by many threats and occasional blows. He was not, it may be readily understood, a popular officer.

In fact, the mate had no friends aboard the steamer, and he wanted none. To the captain he granted a sort of sulky deference, but towards all the others his attitude was that of disagreeable slave driver. The newcomers were no exception to this rule. Indeed he seemed to think it necessary to be particularly harsh to them in order to show them that they must not presume on their status as semi-guests.

For Pieface the mate conceived and cherished a hearty dislike from the first. Dogs, he felt, had absolutely no place aboard ship—or anywhere else. They were of no earthly use except to kick in an excess of rage, and men served that purpose even better than dogs.

Pieface, at first, was unaware of the mate's attitude. Under the influence of the mighty sea he had become mature, and the indiscriminate affectionateness of his puppyhood had been cast away. More and more he became an aloof creature, as he stalked majestically about the deck of the steamer, scorning to make overtures to every man he saw, as he had been wont to do in his more frivolous days. Yet in the same degree that his aloofness to the general run of mankind grew, he became more firmly attached to his little group of chosen friends; and Wilson formerly his enemy, was now recognized as his chosen master. He himself had made the decision, and it was recognized.

Plugugly Peters had been to Pieface but one more man. In his travels over the ship he had met him now and then, but a mutual stare had been the extent of their relationships. In a mild way Pieface had been inclined to look with favor on the mate, because the latter never attempted

to force him into playful antics, as did
some of the other men.

One incident, soon to be followed by others of a similar nature, quickly dispelled
any favor the dog may have been inclined
to bestow, however. He met the mate in
the companionway one day, and, as usual,
paid no more attention than a passing
stare. The mate stared back, not pleasantly.
As they drew near one another, both kept
to the middle of passage. Then, seeing
that one or the other must turn out, Pieface
started to do so. But he was too late. Peters, walking rapidly, bore down on him,
lifted back a heavily-shod foot and planted
it with all his strength under the dog's
body. Pieface was lifted clear and hurled
into the partition.

He yelped in surprised pain as Plugugly
cursed. Then, like a tiger, he turned,
bared his sharp teeth, and started to lunge
at the mate's leg. His teeth sank into the
flesh, and clung there for a fraction of a
second, as Peters brought his other foot
into play. Then the dog released his hold,
and crouched back, waiting. The mate, still

cursing, strode away, and Pieface made no move to follow. It was the first skirmish.

After that affair Pieface studiously avoided the mate as much as possible. But that was not always possible on so small a steamer, and there were other times when the two had encounters of a more or less violent nature. Always, however, Pieface satisfied himself with a hasty snap in retribution for an equally hasty kick or cuff, and then the combatants went their respective ways. But each was getting increasingly angry.

Even as a puppy, ludicrous as he was, Pieface had not been acquainted with fear. Now the new Pieface, mature in mind and body, was not the dog to slink away from the threats of the bullying mate. Yet he had been well trained in the behavior that is expected of the best of his kind, and he knew, subconsciously, that he would displease his young master and his friends by any undue display of belligerency. His anger had not yet risen to such a point as to overcome this influence.

He spent a great deal of time in the companionship of Wilson and Bill Johnson,

knowing that when he was with them nothing unpleasant was likely to happen. If
the mate appeared on these occasions, there
might be loud and blatant words issuing
from his lips, but they were directed at the
men. The dog was ignored.

As on the fishing schooner, too, Pieface
became a privileged guest in the captain's
cabin. He had readily admitted Captain
Carlson into his little circle of favorites,
and the captain had returned the compliment by showing his unstinted friendliness
for the dog. Theirs was a quiet friendship,
the captain being a quiet man, and many
an hour they spent in the cabin together,
each fully conscious of the other's presence,
but with no word from the captain and no
sound from Pieface. The captain would sit
over a book or writing paper at his desk,
and Pieface would lie motionless in a corner until at last the captain rose and ex-
tended a hand in his direction; whereupon
the dog would rise and walk over for an
affectionate pat on the head before following the captain out to some other part of
the ship.

In this way, although Pieface did not

know it, there came to be established over the dog a sort of protectorate. Peters undoubtedly would have carried his ill will to much greater extremes, had he not realized that by so doing he would incur the stern disfavor of his superior officer. For a time this realization was sufficient to curb his temper and cause him to content himself with such minor acts of brutality as would not be found out.

But the nature of the man and the nature of the dog were such that it was inevitable that a conflict should arise between them eventually. It was only a question of which should lose control of himself first. Peters was merely waiting for the right opportunity to give vent to his lust for cruelty without injury to himself. This involved getting the dog in such a condition that he could not retaliate, and also it involved solitude, in order that there might be no retribution from the captain. Pieface, on the other hand, was actuated by no such prudence. He felt the conflict coming on, but was fighting against it with all the will power that he could summon. Involuntarily he growled and bared his teeth when-

ever the mate came in sight. He felt no
dread of the impending conflict—rather he
craved it. Yet he held himself in leash.

It was Pieface who finally threw down
the gauntlet, and at a time when the mate
was unprepared and unconscious of the
dog's presence. Nor was it to satisfy his
own grudge that Pieface went to battle.
Characteristically, he threw his caution to
the winds when his master was made the
object of the mate's brutality.

Wilson had been scrubbing the deck, and
singing as he scrubbed. Scrubbing the
deck is an occupation that is always available on shipboard when there is little else to
do, and the erstwhile young cynic was finding it his chief duty in these days, as the
steamer plowed its way northward. Also,
strangely, he was finding it a pleasant task.
For the metamorphosis in Wilson had been
great. Life was no longer bitter, but sweet.
He no longer brooded over the days when
he had been a lad of leisure, because he had
discovered that there is even greater happiness in work—even such work as he would
formerly have considered degrading. So
he sang as he scrubbed.

And as he scrubbed and sang, Plugugly Peters came up behind him and looked down with his usual unfriendly leer. Wilson, unaware of the mate's presence behind him, scrubbed on, throwing in a flourish here and there by way of accompaniment to his song.

"Shut up and get to work," bellowed the mate, angered, as always, by seeing any one apparently enjoying work. His theory was that any work had to be done sullenly and under compulsion to be effective.

Wilson, surprised by the bellow from behind, stopped in mid-flourish. And as he stopped, his swab snapped in the air. From it flew several drops of rather dirty water, and these, carried by the wind, came to rest full in the mate's face. That face, usually red, turned almost white with rage; Plugugly's huge firsts rose spasmodically over his head; a great roar came from within him.

Shouting inarticulately, he lunged at the startled youth, seized the swab from his hands and threw it across the deck, grabbed Wilson by the scruff of the neck, shook him violently, and then, before Wilson realized what it was all about, landed his startled victim such a blow on the jaw that he fell in a heap on the deck.

It was here that Pieface entered the dispute. He had just been coming in search of Wilson when he saw the mate standing there, and consequently he had remained in the background, still avoiding trouble. But when he saw the mate suddenly rush at his master and knock him down, he had forgotten all his resolutions. All the rage that had been gathering within him was intensified by this assault, and Pieface had no thought but to tear this brute of a man to pieces in as short a time as possible. There would be no mild snapping at the ankles this time.

He leaped, reaching with his teeth for the mate's throat. Instinctively Peters dodged as the dog flashed at him. Pieface's teeth sank harmlessly in the open collar of the mate's shirt; the cloth gave way with a gentle ripping noise; Pieface was carried violently to the deck by the force of his own leap.

Plugugly rushed at him as he fell, and delivered a broadside kick that seemed to

push in every rib, and sent him sliding four
or five feet further across the deck. Peters
drew back his foot to kick again, aiming
this time at the dog's head, but before the
kick landed Pieface was on his feet again,
ready to continue the battle on more even
terms.

He met the oncoming leg squarely, sinking his teeth deep into the calf. Peters
roared with pain and kicked madly, trying
to dislodge the dog. This proving futile, he
sank down on his other knee, and grabbed
the dog's throat, squeezing with all the
force of his two hands. Still Pieface clung
on with his teeth, trying only to sink them
deeper in the flesh. Plugugly tried to yank
himself free, but succeeded only in tearing
his own flesh with Pieface's teeth.

It seemed to be settling down to a con-
test of endurance, Pieface clinging with
his teeth, Peters clinging with his hands,
when the mate suddenly tried new tactics.
Giving up his grip on the dog's throat, he
turned quickly on his side, rolling the dog
under him in an attempt to crush him by
superior weight. He knew that the dog could
not long withstand his choking operations.

but he desired a quicker issue of the conflict, and release from the pain inflicted by
the dog's teeth.

Pieface met the new assault by releasing
his hold on the mate's leg. Peters croaked
with relief. But Pieface was not giving up.
Squirming out from under the mate's huge
body, he gathered himself for a new leap at
his sprawling adversary.

Then Peters did a surprising thing. Instead of rushing at the dog and making
an end to the fight before Pieface could re-
new his attack, he leaped to his feet and
ran down the deck. Pieface, seeing his
antagonist in flight, assumed that victory
was in his grasp, but he had no intention
of leaving it indecisive. He transformed
his intended leap into a dash, and gave
chase.

But the mate suddenly stopped his flight
and turned. And in his hand was an ax.
He had seen it lying on a half-opened pack-
ing case, and it had been the purpose of his
apparent flight. He was ready now to continue the battle on his own terms.

Pieface saw his danger, and stopped before getting in range of the ax. But his

anger was undimmed, and he still sought an opening. He backed away, growling, as the mate advanced upon him. Peters rushed; Pieface dodged. Thus they manouvered back and forth on the deck, keeping out of one another's reach but each waiting for a chance to strike.

Finally Plugugly grew tired of this inaction. With a great oath, he lifted the ax above his head to hurl it at the dog. But as it hovered for a moment over his head, he felt it suddenly wrenched from his grasp. He turned, and Wilson, pale and glassy-eyed, was holding the ax threateningly in his upraised hand.

"You!" yelled the mate, and rage choked further words in his throat.

"I," said Wilson, still holding the ax. He had recovered from the stunning effect of his fall to the deck just in time to seize the uplifted ax before it flew from the mate's hand.

Plugugly found words to express himself at last. They came in a torrent, profane and scorching. Then Pieface rushed at him again.

"No, Pieface. Enough," Wilson commanded.

The dog reluctantly backed away.

The mate, still cursing, left them.

CHAPTER XIV

A NIGHT ATTACK

AFTER the combat Wilson was unde-
cided whether or not to invoke the
captain's protection for the dog. To do so,
he knew, would be to expose the unpleasant
relations existing between himself and the
mate, and he disliked to let the captain
know that his presence or that of Pieface
was causing discord aboard the vessel. Yet
he feared the outcome of another encounter
between the mate and the dog, particularly
if there was nobody present to interfere.
He felt sure that Plugulgy would make
certain of solitude before again coming to
grips with Pieface.

He told the whole story to Bill Johnson,
and the latter agreed with him that it
would be embarrassing to go to the captain
with a complaint so soon.

"I kinder have an idea we can look out
for the old sea-dog, so long as we know

how the land lays," said Bill. "For that matter, I figger he could look out for himself if he was up against anybody that played the game square. As for this feller Plugugly, he'll hang himself if he gets rope enough, as the feller says. All we got to do is see that he don't hang Pieface first."

They agreed to keep a close watch of Pieface's comings and goings, hoping to forestall the attempt on his life which they were inwardly certain the mate would make at the first opportunity.

Meanwhile Pieface went about his business unconcernedly. With the confidence of courage, he felt sure that he could have made an end to the mate if the fight had been allowed to go on, and he had no fear of a fresh encounter. Indeed he even craved a continuation of hostilities, and the very thought of the mate caused him to bristle and growl. Sometimes, while dozing, he would dream that the battle was on again, but his own excitement always awoke him before he had reached the satisfactory end of the dream.

Yet he bided his time. Wilson had talked

to him very seriously after the fight, and he knew that he was forbidden to attack except upon good provocation. And though the sight of Peters drove him nearly frantic with anger, he restrained himself, and again took to avoiding contact with the mate.

Plugugly also bided his time. Pieface's friends by no means overestimated the mate's wrath, and he nursed it day and night. It was the nature of the man to enjoy hate more than any milder emotion, and he gave himself up to a blood thirsty antipathy for the dog that had dared to cross him. He took a savage pleasure in planning the revenge that he was determined to have.

And the crowning touch to the plan, as Plugugly saw it, was the blow Pieface's death would be to Wilson and Bill, whom the mate hated only slightly less than the dog. He was physically incapable of feeling affection himself, but he could recognize it in others, and he knew how deeply he could wound his enemies through the object of their affection. So Plugugly laid his plans.

But he knew that the skipper was growing increasingly fond of the dog, and his plans had to be so much the more crafty. If Pieface suddenly dropped from sight, he, Plugugly, would be the first to be suspected and questioned. He knew that. And he intended to leave no tell tale traces to upset the lie which he would tell. He wanted Wilson and Bill to know that it was he who had killed the dog, and he was certain that they would know it, regardless of how well he might be able to cover his tracks. It would take half the savor out of the deed if he could not mock them and gloat over them. Yet he wanted Captain Carlson to believe him innocent, for he could not afford to lose the captain's favor. He thought he could accomplish all this.

Captain Carlson could not help knowing that Pieface and Plugugly were not friends but he did not imagine the extent of their enmity. He was accustomed to the surly demeanor of his mate, and would have been surprised to find the man getting friendly with the dog: it was no surprise that the opposite should be true. He considered Peters a capable mate, unpleasant as he might be as a man, and he asked no more

of him. If Pieface did not like him, then
Pieface was merely accepting the taste of
everybody on board. And if Peters did
not-like Pieface, then Peters was merely
adding the dog to a list which included
everybody on board. Captain Carlson saw
nothing in the situation to worry him.

Uneventful day followed uneventful day,
as the little steamer plowed sturdily northward. Wilson and Bill, keeping a sharp
lookout for fresh encounter between Pieface and Plugugly, began to wonder if they
were unduly nervous and suspicious. For
nothing happened. The dog proceeded as
his fancy dictated over the whole ship,
sometimes stalking majestically, again gam-
boling like a frisky lamb. But nothing
happened. He was unmolested. Peters
continued surly, but inactive.

One day, indeed, Wilson, carrying a pan
of garbage from the cook's galley, was
alarmed at hearing a sharp series of barks
from another quarter of the vessel. He
dropped the pan with a clatter, and ran at
top speed to the place from which the
sounds had come—only to find Pieface being joyously roughed by the skipper, and

both enjoying themselves vociferously. He
retreated before the captain was aware of
his presence, but when he returned to his
abandoned garbage pan, it was to find
Plugugly standing, feet wide apart, glaring
at him and the mass on the deck alternately.
He took the mate's cuff on the head without
a murmur, and cleaned up the unsavory
mess, too much relieved by the falseness of
his fears to be angry.

"I am beginning to think our excitement
has been wasted," said Wilson, after telling
Bill about the incident.

"Well, Plugugly stays ugly enough, but
he don't seem to be doin' much pluggin' for
a fact," admitted the fisherman. "Still, I
ain't takin' him to my manly bosom yet
awhile."

"Maybe he has decided to let well enough
alone."

"If you mean he's afraid to tackle Pieface again, you don't know the gent, son.
He's a dark customer, that feller."

"Well, he must be afraid of something
or somebody," reasoned Wilson, "or he
would have killed Pieface long ago. He
certainly hates him enough—and us, too."

"Maybe," said Bill, considering the matter for a moment. "He ain't afraid of the dog, though, and he ain't afraid of you and me. 'Course there's the skipper."

"I think that's it," Wilson quickly agreed.

"More'n likely," said Bill. "Still he'll bear watchin' a while longer."

Wilson agreed, and the watch continued, but still nothing happened. Thus gradually they relaxed their guard—which was exactly what Plugugly was waiting for. Each succeeding day increased their optimism and decreased their misgivings. The mate was going about his business in his usual surly manner. He swore and cuffed and raged, but that was all. Had he become mild or propitiatory, he would have aroused new suspicions; by maintaining his accustomed rôle, without getting actually violent he disarmed suspicion.

He was waiting, planning, scheming. His hour would strike, and the longer he had to wait for it, the sweeter would be his revenge. He saw Pieface being allowed more and more to remain out of the sight of Wilson and Bill, and he congratulated him-

self on his strategy. His hour would strike
—and soon.

At length Pieface played directly into
his hands. It was a pitch-dark night. The
day had been thick and muggy, and Pieface
had spent most of it in sleeping, his favorite
companions being too busy to play with
him. Thus when night came, the dog had
found himself surfeited with sleep. He
decided on a nocturnal prowl about the ship.

He slipped out of his bunk and made
his way on deck. Back in the stern he could
hear the footfalls of the watch. There was
no other sound except the lapping of the
sea against the prow and sides of the
steamer and the monotonous chugging of
the engine. Pieface stood quite still for a
moment, trying to decide how best he might
amuse himself.

His first thought was to make his presence known to the man on watch, and thus
gain a companion in sport. He made a
move to do this, but stopped as another idea
came to him. He would pretend that the
watch was an enemy to be trailed and
stalked down. That would be a good game
for a while. Later he could announce him-

self and proceed with his original plan. He slipped behind a bulkhead in pursuance of his game.

The watch proceeded forward with deliberate, contemplative steps. Pieface, leaping from shadow to shadow, followed, unseen. His heart pounded with excitement; his eyes sparkled in the darkness with the zest of the sport. Only the realization that it would spoil the game held back the joyful yelp that his throat ached to utter. His wagging tail belied the apparent ferocity of his attitude.

So forward, and then back astern again, dodging, hiding, following. The unsuspecting watch paused in his methodical step, and gave vent to a great yawn, stretching himself. Pieface crouched, quivering with delightful excitement. It was nearly time, he decided, to leap out of the darkness and announce himself. What a roaring and barking he would muster up for that supreme moment!

Then a new idea came to him. He would let the watch get a long start on him. By doing so he would have a long run to overtake him, thus prolonging the sport and allowing more time for the full enjoyment of the thousand barks he had welled up within him. So he remained still while the watch plodded away from him.

Thoroughly absorbed in his game, Pie-face had no place in his mind or senses for other things. Yet now, as the sound of the watch's steps was lost in the distant darkness, he became vaguely aware of some new element entering the game. He heard nothing definite; perhaps it was a new odor; or perhaps it was merely a feeling, an instinct. At any rate, he stiffened expectantly.

But even as he stiffened, there was a lunge through the darkness, and two vice-like hands settled over his throat. A low human growl sounded in his ears, and he knew that the game had become a deadly serious affair. It was Plugugly. He wrenched and struggled. He tried to squirm about so as to get his teeth into action. He tried to bark. But it was all in vain. The mate's great hands held him off and effectually choked all his cries before they were uttered.

Now his assailant dragged him bodily toward the rail, never for a moment releas-

ing the death grip on his throat. Pieface
contested every foot of the way, but his
efforts were futile. The carefully-laid plans
of the mate were working to perfection.
Nearer and nearer the rail. Nearer and
nearer—

Somewhere in the darkness Pieface again
heard the footsteps of the watch. If he
could only make that unsuspecting playmate hear him now, as he had planned to do
a few minutes before. He squirmed might-
ily again, and for just a second he felt the
grasp about his throat loosen. With all his
lung power he yelped. It was just a small
fraction of a yelp in duration, but a full-
blown yelp in volume. Plugugly's hands
squeezed with new strength to cut it off.

The mate cursed softly in the dog's ear.
"No, you don't," said he. "You'll be overboard before you yip again."

The watch evidently stopped at the sound
of the dog's stifled cry, for his steps were
no longer audible. But soon they were
heard again, getting closer, and the mate
yanked the dog bodily into the air by the
throat. They were now close to the rail.

Another few steps, and Pieface would disappear over the side.

But now a new step was added to that of the watch.

"Hulloa, watch," came a voice. It was the skipper's.

"Hulloa," came the answering cry.

A light shone through the darkness, and revealed the watch, waiting for the captain's next word. Its rays did not strike the mate and the dog, however.

"What was that cry?" asked the captain.

"Don't know, sir," said the watch. "I was lookin' around to find out."

Plugugly moved toward the rail, but quietly. He could not afford to be found out now.

Suddenly the captain's light swept around the deck in an arc. The mate, seeing it coming, attempted to finish his job before being seen, but the light struck him just as he poised the dog over the rail. The captain yelled an incoherent command. The mate straightened up, and dropped the dog. Pieface lay unconscious on the deck.

"So," said the captain, approaching the

mate, and looking down at the unconscious figure at his feet.

Plugugly stood still, surly as ever.

The captain stared at his underofficer, his face expressionless. Then he looked down again at the dog, which was shivering a little now and gasping for breath. The captain's face twitched. Without a word and without seeming to make any preparation, he drew back his arm and struck the mate squarely in the face. The mate half stumbled, and made as though to defend himself. But the captain merely took a step forward and swung again. Peters went sprawling on the deck, and lay there.

"Now get below. You won't get off so easy another time," said the captain.

He picked up Pieface gently in his arms, and carried him to his own cabin.

A few minutes later Plugugly scrambled to his feet and slunk below.

CHAPTER XV

INTO THE NORTH

THE providential appearance of Captain Carlson while Peters and Pieface were struggling did more than put an end to that particular encounter. It opened the eyes of the captain to his mate's state of mind, and put Pieface definitely under his protectorate. The following day he called Peters into his cabin, and told him in no uncertain terms to leave the dog alone. And Peters knew better than to defy the skipper.

Pieface was not at all appreciative of this intervention. The fact that he been twice at the point of death at Plugugly's hands made no impression on him. He still believed blindly that he could conquer his enemy if the struggle between them was allowed to be resumed. That it was not allowed to be resumed was a great disappointment to him, now that his fighting blood was up.

He felt justified now in starting the
next fight himself, and had he found an
opportunity he would have leaped on the
mate. But the opportunity did not come.
Peters avoided him, as he had avoided Peters in the past. One or two ineffectual attempts he made to turn his plans into action, but his only reward for his trouble was
a hurried kick in the ribs and the sight of
Plugugly retreating out of his reach.

Gradually, in the face of such disappointment, Pieface's blood cooled, and he resumed his calmer manner of life aboard
ship. For a time the lust for battle had
entirely filled him, so that everything else
was but as a dim memory in his mind. Now
however, he found himself again conscious
of the possibilities of happiness in his en-
vironment. Once more he felt himself
glorying in the tang of the sea air, the
pleasant rolling of the steamer, the companionship of his chosen coterie of friends.
Once he dreamed of being in the green
fields of Miquelon, and he was terribly unhappy about it. It was a great relief to awake
and find himself safely on shipboard, with

the sound of the beating waves in his ears.
He had been weaned of the land.

The steamer was getting well away from
civilization. Sydney, Nova Scotia, the last
real outpost, had been visited for a final
taking-on of supplies; for several days now
the ship had been pushing steadily through
the bleak waters of Hudson Strait.

Wilson, as well as Pieface, had become
thoroughly acclimated to the life on shipboard, and he was beginning to learn many
of the rudiments of navigation. In his
marine education he benefitted not only by
the tutelage of Bill, but also by that of
Captain Carlson, who took a more and
more fatherly interest in him as the days
went by.

To Picface belonged most of the credit
for this friendship, for the skipper, craving
companionship, sought the dog out often,
and usually found him in the company of
Wilson. Thus he fell into the habit of inviting Wilson to come and talk with him in
his cabin—and bring the dog with him.
Wilson, though his newly-awakened pride
would not have allowed him to curry the
captain's favor, was glad enough to have

it given to him unsought, and he soon
came to look forward eagerly to what the
captain called their "gab sessions."

They talked at first mostly of Pieface,
since it was in the dog that they found
their first and chief mutual interest. And
this was very pleasant for Pieface, too,
because he would sit between them and listen to their voices, conscious of the fact
that he was being discussed, even if he did
not know what was being said about him.
Occasionally he would try to break into
the conversation, particularly if he heard
his name mentioned or caught an intonation
that pleased him. Such conversational outbreaks on his part were usually accepted
with entire solemnity by his companions,
and fitting answers were made to him,
greatly to his satisfaction.

But the present virtues of even as estim-
able a dog as Pieface could not last as a
conversational topic forever, and gradually
the skipper began to lead Wilson into telling of the dog's history. Wilson replied
guardedly at first, telling only snatches
here and there, as a more detailed account
would necessarily involve his own life's

story. This he hesitated still to divulge, partly from reluctance to appear boastful; more because he was ashamed of a great part of it.

Little by little, however, as his friendship and respect for the captain increased, he began to talk about himself. And the captain, paying close attention at such moments, plied him with questions, most of which he still evaded.

Then, one day, Wilson made some reference to big ocean liners, while discussing ships in general.

"You've been across?" asked Captain Carlson.

"Yes."

"As a passenger?"

Wilson realized that he had opened up the field of his past life again, but he saw no retreating. "Yes," he said.

"Tell me, Wilson," said Captain Carlson. "Aren't you the son of John Bersey?"

Wilson fidgeted, then, in a low voice, said, "Yes."

"I thought so," said the skipper.

Wilson looked steadfastly down at Pie·

face, and nervously rubbed the dog's head. The captain watched him speculatively.

"How do you happen to be here, Wilson? Won't you tell me?"

Hesitantly the boy told his story, emphasizing his own wretched state of mind before he was taken aboard the fishing schooner, and pleading with the captain to believe in the sincerity of his change of heart.

The captain listened sympathetically, muttering, "Yes, yes," in an encouraging voice whenever Wilson seemed to falter.

"You don't need to tell me that you've changed, Wilson," he said, when the story was finished. "The part I find hard to believe is that you ever were as bad as you say you were. I should never have believed that you and Pieface were anything but the best of pals."

As he spoke, the dog rubbed against Wilson's leg, and stuck his head up to be scratched.

"No, sir, I never should have believed it," repeated the captain.

Then: "So John Bersey is dead? Lad, there was a wonderful man, your father.

I brought some dogs into Miquelon for him when he was first starting his kennels there. I got to know and to like him, both of us being sort of partial to dogs, and I used to call in on him whenever I could. A wonderful man, wasn't he, Pieface?"

Pieface, who would have been the first to agree with this sentiment had he known what it was, barked lustily, and crossed over to let the captain fondle him.

Wilson's confession made the bond between him and the captain all the stronger, and the latter devoted more and more hours to instructing the youth in navigation and the business of shipping. Thus Wilson learned that they were now heading for a trading post in Repulse Bay, a northern arm of Hudson Bay on the very edge of the Arctic Circle. This would be the northernmost point touched by the vessel, and from there it would work south, stopping at the other trading posts on its line as it returned.

The steamer sailed on through the strait, through Fox Channel and into Repulse Bay. As it was summer, the northern weather was pleasant, though fog hovered about the ship most of the time, making it impossible to see much more than the familiar things of the vessel itself.

It was a clear day, however, when the ship hove in sight of the trading post. Seven little buildings were clustered on the rocky shore. Around these was a fringe of skin tents. Riding at anchor outside were a small schooner, a sailing vessel, and a number of smaller boats. Figures moved about, enlivening the scene—the first human beings except those on the ship that the crew of the "Sturdy" had seen since leaving Sydney.

Pieface, poising himself on the bridge beside Captain Carlson, barked an excited welcome as his eyes fell on this scene. And though his barks floated hopelessly into the air, they seemed to him to create a response, for on the shore the moving figures were increasing and all were moving about excitedly.

The steamer drew closer and anchored. A half dozen Eskimo boats raced with one another to reach her side, and hardly had the anchor been dropped and a ladder thrown overside before the Eskimos were clambering aboard. Captain Carlson welcomed them with a hearty grin and both hands full of tobacco. The latter he tossed to them as they climbed aboard, and they grasped it greedily, shouting their thanks like children.

Two of the Eskimos, older than the rest and with wizened-up faces, the captain greeted with particular ceremony, talking with them in their own tongue. Wilson, watching with interest, noted a shadow come over the captain's face as he talked, and then saw him lead the two old men below to his cabin. For a moment he pondered over the question of what bad news the captain could have been hearing, but then his attention was diverted by Pieface.

The dog at first had looked askance at these outlanders. He had not been quite sure whether to welcome them or drive them away. He had tried a few experimental barks to find out whether or not they were easily frightened, but discovering that they took no notice of these sallies he had decided that their consciences must be clear and that they were therefore deserving of civility. Approaching one of the youngest of the Eskimos, he had sniffed inquiringly, and had been enchanted by the rather greasy odor that he had found. Immedi- ately he had accepted the Eskimo lad as a friend, and it was their exchange of good will that had attracted Wilson's attention.

Pieface was leaping up and down, bark- ing and pawing at the Eskimo lad, while the latter was clapping his hands and jab- bering with glee. Having lived all his life in a country where dogs are essential to life as the only means of overland transpor- tation, yet the Eskimo had never seen a dog of Pieface's breed before. He was familiar only with the great huskies that pull the sleds of the North. Pieface, there- fore, was as strange to him as he was to Pieface, and both of them were greatly ex- cited by their discoveries.

Wilson stood for a few minutes watch- ing their antics. Then, as they hopped about the deck, they drew nearer to him. After a while, as Pieface leaped playfully backward, his eyes still on the Eskimo, he bumped full into Wilson. He turned to see who it was, and recognizing his chosen master, turned and jumped up, putting his forepaws on Wilson's body.

The Eskimo lad, seeing that he had been deserted, stood still, grinning. Wilson grinned back, patting Pieface on the head. Then, not knowing how to talk to the Eskimo, he held out his hand. The Eskimo lad understood the gesture, and shook hands, saying something in his own language, to which Wilson shook his head uncomprehendingly. Pieface, delighted to see Wilson apparently approving his new friend, dropped to the deck and shook his tail enthusiastically.

Having shaken hands, Wilson was at a loss how to continue the companionship. He turned to the dog again, and clapped his hands together.

"Pieface," he said.

Pieface looked up at him and barked. Wilson again grinned at the Eskimo lad, then pointed his finger at the dog and repeated his name.

"Pieface."

The Eskimo nodded.

"Piefess," he said, and when the dog responded he grinned all the more, well pleased with himself at having learned an English name.

Wilson decided to try introducing himself by the same method.

"Wilson," he said, pointing his finger at his own breast.

The Eskimo looked interested but uncertain.

Wilson repeated the word and gesture several times, while his new friend made experimental moves with his lips. Finally he seemed satisfied.

"Oo-illson," he said.

Wilson nodded, and they both laughed and shook hands again. Then Wilson pointed at the Eskimo, and lifted his eyebrows inquiringly. The Eskimo understood the question, and pointed his own finger at himself, as Wilson had done.

"Soolak," he said.

"Soolak," repeated Wilson, and again they shook hands, as Pieface leaped up and demanded a share of their attention.

Just then Plugugly Peters came near, and the dog stiffened and uttered a low growl. Wilson stroked his head, and spoke to him in a soothing voice. Soolak looked surprised.

The mate stopped to talk to a deckhand, and as he talked Captain Carlson came on deck again, followed by the two old Eskimos with whom he had been talking.

"Peters," said the captain, "near as I can make out from what these two men tell me, Sanderson, our trader, has gone crazy. They say he is a medicine man now, and from the way they describe the things he is doing, I know something must be wrong with his head. All I see to do is to go ashore and find out about it and see if I can straighten things out. You are in charge until I come back."

"Yes, sir," said the mate.

Wilson, overhearing the conversation, looked apprehensively at Pieface, then at Plugugly. As he looked at the latter, he met his eyes, and the look in them was not at all reassuring. But Pieface also had seen the mate look in his direction, and his reaction was a fierce growl.

At the sound of it the captain, who was just about to have a boat lowered, turned quickly on his heel.

"Oh, Peters," he said.

"Yes, sir "

"See that nothing happens to that dog while I'm gone. I'm rather fond of him."

"Yes, sir," said the mate.

But the look of triumph was still in his eye when the captain descended into the waiting boat.

CHAPTER XVI

THE HUSKY

THE men on the "Sturdy" were more curious than excited over the outcome of the captain's trip ashore. Most of them were seasoned seafaring men, and were accustomed to seeing strange things happen in the far corners of the world. Thus it occasioned them little surpise to learn that the trader, after long months in the North had lost his mind.

They discussed it in little groups around the deck, telling one another sagely of the things that bring on insanity in such cases —lonesomeness, longing, monotony. Some of them, exhausting the realm of speculation, fell into reminiscence and told one another of similar things that had happened in this or that remote part of the globe. One had been on a ship which had brought a crazed missionary home from the African coast; another, stranded with a shipmate on a South Sea island, had seen his companion gradually revert to the savagery of a madman; even Bill Johnson had a tale to tell of a Portuguese fisherman who had been lost in a dory and who had gone mad with fear before he was rescued.

Wilson listened to these stories with awe and wonder, and the story-tellers, noting with satisfaction that they had a good listener, doubtless added to their stories a few embellishments that they had never thought about before.

"If I were going into a place like that to stay," said Wilson, nodding his head toward the Eskimo settlement, "I'd take Pieface with me to keep me company."

He stetched out his hand and stroked the dog's head. "You wouldn't let me go crazy would you, old boy?"

"Maybe he wouldn't," one of the story-tellers replied, "but it seems to me that if dogs could keep a man in his right mind, this-here trader had ought to have been all-right. Look there."

He pointed to the shore, where at least half a dozen big, shaggy dogs could be seen moving to and fro with wolf-like steps.

"And those are real he-dogs, too," he added. "Not but what I like this little feller here all right, you understand, but one of those huskies could eat him up for breakfast most any morning."

Plugugly Peters, striding sullenly by as this remark was made, seemed to have a mental picture of the meal described, for he looked appreciatively at the huskies on shore, then back at the terrier, and the expression on his face was as near a grin as the face was capable of attaining.

Pieface, beyond a doubt, would have been outraged at the suggestion if he had knowr what it was, but being blissfully ignorant of the slur cast on his ability to protect his carcass, he strolled nonchalantly about the deck with his usual cocky air. Mounting a bulkhead, he caught a glimpse of the dogs on shore, and as though to show that he, at least, had no fears of the outcome of a battle, barked challengingly. The dogs on shore, failing to hear the futile barking of the terrier, paid not the slightest attention though Pieface barked and barked, furious at being unable to ruffle the calm of the huskies.

"That's a good safe place to bark from," laughed the sailor who had belittled Pieface's chances in an encounter with an Eskimo dog. "Better not bark too loud, though, or one of those huskies will hear you and swim out and eat you up."

"I guess it wouldn't be such a lark, even for a husky," said Wilson feeling that loyalty demanded that he come to the dog's defence.

"Still I wouldn't be promoting a match, if I were you," replied the doleful sailor.

"I won't," Wilson promised.

As the day wore on and the captain did not return, the curiosity of the men grew more and more keen. The conversation of the little groups returned from the far fields into which it had strayed to the increasingly interesting topic immediately at hand. It had been expected that the captain would be back within a few hours at the most, either with the trader or with assurance that the story of the Eskimos was untrue. But the entire afternoon had passed, and night was coming on, and the captain was still away. Wilson feared that some mischance had occurred, and he confided his fears to

some of the men, but they only scoffed at
him.   The captain was all right, they assured him but he must have found something interesting to keep him ashore so long.
Speculation as to what it was that he had
found occupied the minds of the men, and
they talked on, suggesting all sorts of weird
possibilities to each other.

Finally, as night fell, an Eskimo boat
put out from shore and drew alongside the
steamer. The men, wondering what tidings
its occupant brought, crowded to the rail as
the Eskimo boatman climbed aboard. But
their curiosity was not to be satisfied. Peters also had seen the boat, and he was waiting when the message-bearer reached the
deck. Glaring around him, as though chal-
lenging any one to come a step nearer or
to question his authority in any way, he
took a note from the Eskimo, scanned it,
crammed it in his pocket, nodded a dismissal to the Eskimo, and turned on his heel.

The men stood back silently as the mate
strode, away, but Pieface, less of wary of
his safety, stiffened, sniffed, and uttered a
low growl—a warning growl that he could
not suppress. Plugugly looked at the dog,

and made no move in recognition of the growl except to continue as he was going, but once more there was spread over his face the near-grin that had been there earlier in the day when the sailor had been talking about the imaginative encounter between Pieface and a husky.

"What a fine guy he is," muttered one of the deck hands as Peters disappeared below.

"Yeh," said another. "You'd think he might at least give us an idea of what the old man's doin' ashore."

"Guess he's not comin' back to-night, anyhow," put in Bill Johnson. "He wouldn't have bothered to send a note if he was."

The others agreed with him in chorus.

Bill's prophecy proved correct, and morning came with Peters still in command of the ship. About noon he approached Wilson and Bill, who were talking together, with Pieface, as usual, listening to their conversation with an interested air.

"See here," said the mate, "you two get on my nerve, and you know it, and that lousy mutt gets on it more. Take a boat and row yourselves ashore or anywhere out

of my sight for the rest of the afternoon.
And don't leave the dog behind you or you
won't find him when you get back."

He walked away, scowling, while Bill and
Wilson looked at each other in astonishment.

"H'm," said the fisherman, "what's his
game now? He hates us so bad he's givin'
us shore leave, which is sure one funny
way to show a bad temper."

"Shall we go?" asked Wilson.

"We got our orders, and I don't see but
it's a case of go whether we want to or
not," replied Bill. "And as for me, I don't
know as I crave to see Plugugly's face
anymore'n he craves to see mine. Still it
sounds kinder fishy to me, this lettin' us go
ashore jest so he won't have to look at us."

"Do you suppose he has some new scheme
against Pieface?"

"I dunno. I admit I'm stumped. He
must have something up his sleeve, but I
can't figger what it is. Leastways, I don't
see as any harm can come to Pieface if
he's along with us. If we was to leave him
behind, now, it might be another story, or

if we was goin' to send him off somewhere
without you and me along."

"Oh, well," said Wilson, "maybe it's only
as he said. Maybe he does just want to
get us out of his sight for a while. If that
is all there is to it, I'm quite ready to
oblige."

"Me too, boy, but I mistrust that ain't
all. Still I don't see as there's anything
to do but take our little unexpected vacation and be thankful for it, keeping our
eyes open all the while regardless."

Accordingly Bill and Wilson lowered a
boat, with Pieface in it, and set forth to ex-
plore the trading post. Both were frankly
curious to see what the place looked like
and how the natives lived, and even more
curious to learn what had become of Captain Carlson. Thinking of these things as
they rowed ashore, they all but forgot their
misapprehensions about the mate's purpose
in sending them away from the steamer.

Pieface, perched in the bow of the boat,
saw the shore line getting nearer, and be-
trayed considerable excitement at the prospect of setting foot on land again. Though
he was now thoroughly seagoing in his

tastes, he was like all sailors in being pleased at the prospect of a brief sojourn ashore. He showed his anticipatory pleasure by jumping up on the rail and down again every few minutes, and by barking first at the settlement in front of him and then at his companions behind him. The latter, sharing his excitement, laughed at his impatience even as they rowed the faster in their own impatience.

The dog was the first to land as the boat struck the shore. Poised in the bow, he waited only for the dry land to be within jumping distance, and then he leaped. He scampered up and down in joyful abandon as Bill and Wilson jumped out and pulled the boat up on shore.

Hardly had the boat been safely beached however, before Pieface's attitude changed from joyful abandon to tense watchfulness. Stopping stock-still, he stiffened and sniffed peering in the direction of the nearest building, around the corner of which there presently appeared another dog—a big husky— sullen, self-confident, and uncompromising.

The pampered Pieface of a few months ago would have trotted to meet the new comer, glad of the chance to gain a possible playmate; but of late life had become something more than a perpetual play hour, and he had learned that all the world was not as good-natured as John Bersey and Joe Kirkup. Therefore he obeyed the newly-developed instinct of caution, and waited to see what this new dog wanted. If it wanted to romp, Pieface was ready; if it wanted rougher sport, Pieface was not above that either. He stood his ground.

The big husky loped steadily forward, impassive as a great army tank moving into the enemy's territory. Then, within a few feet of the terrier, he stopped, crouched, and uttered a low, fierce growl, as though announcing his intention to drive the terrier back to sea at once, or make an end to him then and there. He swung his head slowly from side to side, like a great lion about to charge; the lust of battle shone in his eyes; growling, he bared his wolf-like fangs, and his powerful muscles, hardened by many long miles in the sledge harness, rippled under his shaggy coat as he crouched. Pieface remained motionless.

All this Bill and Wilson saw as they

turned from pulling the boat up, and for a minute or two they stood still watching, half hypnotized by the power of the primitive passion shining in the eyes of the two dogs. Then, as though suddenly realizing that this awe-inspiring pantomine would soon turn into a bloody battle scene unless something were done about it, Wilson flung himself forward with a shout.

"Here, Pieface. Come here."

But he was too late. It was as though his shout had been the signal for hostilities to commence, and before the words were well out of his mouth, the husky had leaped forward. In a second the two dogs were a blurred mass, revolving, yelping. Wilson, with Bill now close behind him, tried vainly to reach the terrier and pull him out of harm's way, but it was like chasing a ball of lightning, so furiously did the fight proceed.

The bull terrier has few equals as a fighting dog, and Pieface had all the skill and tenacity of his kind. Yet the great husky was more than a fighting dog. He was a veritable volcano, irresistible and overpowering. No dog retains the ferocious and cunning characteristics of the wolf as does the husky, and yet this half-wild beast is used as a beast of burden, thus developing still further his sinewy body, over which is such a shaggy coat of fur that it is next to impossible for another dog to penetrate it with its teeth. Such was Pieface's adversary, half-wild, powerful, almost impregnable.

The husky adopted a slashing attack, snapping at Pieface with his sharp fangs, trying to rip him open. But Pieface fought with the cool confidence born of generations of fighting dogs. Like a skilled boxer, he dodged, side-stepped, and parried, snapping and slashing when the opportunity presented itself, but waiting for the right opening to set his teeth in the grip that has made the terrier the symbol of tenacity.

Once, with a snarl of triumph, he struck his teeth at the husky's throat, but they only closed on a great, choking mass of fur, and before he could resume the defensive a great gash had been torn open in his own throat, and the blood streamed out on the ground. After that he fought more cautiously, and was rewarded by getting an opportunity to splinter one of the forelegs of his opponent with his steel-like jaws, but every time he sought a more vital spot the shaggy fur baffled him and choked him. Meanwhile the growling husky charged and shot back like a battering ram, slashing, slashing, slashing. The injured foreleg slowed him up only for an instant, and then he resumed his tactics again, dragging it under him as though it were of no consequence. Again and again Pieface shot his jaw at the furry throat, but to no avail. And little by little the husky was tearing his hide into ribbons.

All the time the fight had been going on Wilson and Bill had been jumping around frantically, trying to find a way to pull the combatants apart. But so fast and furious had been the fight that neither had been quick enough to get a firm grasp on either dog. After a while Wilson had found a club, and had poised it to strike the husky but every time he lifted it the dogs had shifted positions before he was ready to strike the blow, and he had been as helpless with it as without. Once he had landed a glancing blow on the husky's flank, but it had been apparently unnoticed. And once he had aimed at the husky only to have the club come down on Pieface as the dogs whirled about. That ended his attempts to stop the fight with the club.

At length, however, with Pieface growing constantly weaker from loss of blood—though no whit undaunted—the husky changed his tactics and adopted Pieface's own method. Charging as though to slash again at the terrier's throat, he suddenly sank his teeth into the flesh and clung on, intent on finishing the fight in complete victory. The gallant terrier yanked and squirmed, heedless of the pain these efforts to free himself caused, and determined to continue the fight or die trying.

This change of method on the husky's part, however, opened the way for Pieface's friends. Bill Johnson saw the opening, and seizing a small, stout stick he plunged the end of it between the husky's jaws. Wilson immediately understood what his friend was trying to do, and as Bill loosened the husky's death-grip, he grabbed Pieface with both hands and pulled him away, still struggling. The husky, finding himself baffled, prepared to lunge again, but Bill beat him away with the stick as Wilson whirled Pieface around and interposed his own body between the two dogs. With a final blow at the husky, Bill turned and joined Wilson. Together they picked up the mangled terrier in their arms and carried him to the boat.

Wilson's coat made an impromptu bed in the bottom of the boat, and on it Pieface lay moaning as they rowed back toward the steamer. Wilson talked to him soothingly, but Bill remained silent, his face stern.

"The skunk," he said, at last.

"Who?" asked Wilson.

"Peters."

"Peters?"

"Remember last night when that feller was talking about how a husky would eat Pieface up? Remember Peters goin' by and grinnin'? He knew there'd be a fight; that's why he had us take Pieface ashore. The skunk!"

"I'll bet you're right," said Wilson.

" 'Course I'm right. Look there."

Bill pointed to the steamer. The mate

stood at the rail. He was looking down into the bottom of the boat, where Pieface lay, and a triumphant leer overspread his face.

CHAPTER XVII

THE MEDICINE MAN

PLUGUGLY Peters was disappointed.
And in no mood was Plugugly Peters
less amiable than in disappointment. It
galled him and stung him. It made him
feel that he was not powerful enough to get
what he wanted, and to assuage the bitterness he became so much the more overbear-
ing toward those over whom he did have
power.

The cause of his disappointment was that
Pieface, though mangled, had been brought
back to the ship alive. Hating the dog with
unreasoning hatred, he had thought he saw
the way to be rid of him without prejudice
to himself, but the job had been only half-
done. He knew the natural ferocity of the
half-domesticated Eskimo dogs, and he had
felt certain that if Pieface ever set foot on
land the first dog he met would kill him. He
had hoped that the meeting would not take

place until after Pieface had rambled away from Wilson and Bill. But there his calculations had failed. The meeting had taken place, and the outcome would have been just as he had planned if the man and boy had not been right on the spot at the time to interfere. Well, it was just one more thing to hold against those two. His day would come. And as for the dog—

Just what terrible vengence he would visit on the dog he failed to decide just then, for he was disturbed in his cogitations by shouts on deck. He had been sitting in his cabin ever since the return of Bill, Wilson, and Pieface, his head in his hands, planning ways to get even. Now, however, he arose and went on deck to find out the cause of the shouting.

The men were all lined up at the rail, and a boat was approaching the steamer. Plugugly recognized it at once as the captain's boat. In addition to the captain and the oarsmen there was another man in the boat. This, the mate decided, must be the crazed trader. The captain's trip inland, of which the note had informed him, must have been successful.

This did not please the mate. He had dreamed of the captain getting lost, or being murdered by the crazy man. In that case he would have been in full charge of the steamer, with full power to do as he pleased with any supercargo that might be aboard—such as a dog. In fact he had turned over this possibility in his mind so much that it almost seemed likely to become an actuality. And now the captain was returning, and all his imaginative schemes were come to nought.

Thus was his disappointment increased.

Sanderson, the trader, was a large man, but his gait was faltering, and his face—or that part of it which was not covered with unkempt beard—was haggard and sunken. His vacant, roving eyes shone with madness, and he talked incoherently, gesticulating as he talked. Wilson shivered involuntarily as the man passed him, following the captain below.

Peters also went below, to make his report to the captain. This meant the surrender of his authority and added to his irritability. As usual, however, he displayed no part of his feelings before the captain, but maintained an expressionless face during his brief recital of events.

"How about the dog? Is he all right?" asked the captain when the mate had finished.

"Oh, I believe he got in some kind of a fight ashore this afternoon," Peters replied, as though the whole thing had slipped his mind until that moment.

"Ashore? I thought I told you to see that nothing happened to him," said the captain sternly.

"Yes, sir. You did, sir," replied the mate. "But I saw no harm in letting Johnson and young Bersey take him ashore for bit if they wanted to. I didn't know they were going to match him against an Eskimo dog in a fight. They'd ought to known he'd get beaten."

"You mean to tell me this fight was staged by Johnson and Bersey. You're lying, Peters.

Peters, seeing that he could not make the captain believe the story he had planned to tell, hastily determined to save his own face. "Oh, I really don't know anything about it, sir. I just took it for granted they put on the fight purposely. Maybe it just happened. I don't know. All I know is the dog went ashore with them two and came back all chewed up."

"Peters," said the captain, "I think you are so mean yourself you think everybody else is just the same. You saw the dog had been in a fight, and you took it for granted Johnson and Bersey started the fight. Why, they'd no more let that dog run afoul of a husky than they'd jump overboard. Is he hurt bad?"

"Don't know, sir," said Peters, nearly choking with repressed anger.

"Send Bersey to me."

"Yes, sir."

With this dismissal the captain turned to Sanderson, who was muttering to himself on a bunk. Peters left the cabin calmly enough, although inwardly he was burning with wrath. He found Wilson, and with a curt word ordered him to report to the captain.

The captain was talking to Sanderson when Wilson entered the cabin.

"You can't stay here, Sanderson," he

was saying, "I've got to take you back to the States."

"Ah, but my people," protested the madman in a sepulchral voice, waving his two hands in the air. "What will become of my poor people? I—I, alone, have the power to save them from the evil spirits."

He lowered his voice to a hoarse whisper and continued, "I am Rawkaw the Mighty."

"Sanderson," said the captain, firmly, "listen to me. You are John Sanderson, the trader, and your people are white people in the States. I am going to take you back to them. These Eskimos are not your people, and you are not Rawkaw the Mighty."

A hideous, piercing scream issued from Sanderson's throat, and he half rose, but sank back on the bunk again under the spell of the captain's compelling gaze. "I am Rawkaw the Mighty," he repeated, assuming an air of offended dignity. Then he fell to muttering again.

Captain Carlson turned to Wilson, who had been standing awestruck at the door. "Come in, my boy," he said, reassuringly.

As Wilson entered and seated himself, however, the captain's expression became stern. "What's this I hear about Pieface?" he asked.

"A big husky attached him and almost killed him before Bill and I could get them apart," replied Wilson.

"Just a minute now, Wilson. Did the husky attack him or did you set him on the husky?"

Wilson's astonishment at the question was too genuine to leave any need for further questioning on that score. "All right, all right," said the captain, as the boy remained speechless. "I didn't believe it anyway, but I wanted to be sure. Now tell me, how did you happen to take the dog ashore in the first place. Didn't you know that he would be the prey of the first husky he met?"

"Why, no, we never thought of that. Peters told us to go ashore and take the dog with us, and so we went. That's all."

"Peters told you to do that?"

"Why, yes. He said he was tired of seeing our faces, and the dog's too."

"So?" said the captain, pausing a moment reflectively.

"How's Pieface now?" he asked, at length.

"Pretty cruelly hurt, sir," Wilson replied. "He's in my bunk."

"Why not bring him in here? I'll fix him up a bed in the corner, and see that he's kept comfortable."

"All right," said Wilson.

"And by the way," said the captain, as Wilson started to leave, "find Peters again and ask him to come here, will you?"

"Yes, sir," said Wilson.

After carrying the message to the mate, Wilson went to his bunk for Picface. The dog looked up appreciatively as Wilson approached, and sighed.

"You've got to be moved, old boy," said Wilson.

Pieface essayed a weak bark in response.

Wilson started to pick him up in his arms, but at this Pieface protested. Understanding then that he was to be taken from the bunk, he insisted on moving under his own locomotion. Wilson, respecting his grit, set him down and allowed him to limp along behind him.

Peters was just ahead of them as they arrived at the door of the captain's cabin. He scowled angrily at them as he preceded them into the cabin, but his face was once more expressionless as soon as he had passed into the captain's presence.

"Did you send for me, sir?" he asked, ignoring the presence of Wilson and Pieface.

"Yes," the captain replied briefly, brushing past him to meet the dog and examine his wounds. Then, leaving the mate fidgeting in wounded dignity, he proceeded to make the dog comfortable in the bed he had prepared for him.

Pieface settled down with a sigh of contentment in his new bed. He tried feebly to thank the captain for his trouble, but found the effort beyond his strength, and closed his eyes for a snooze.

Then the captain turned to Plugugly, who was trying to appear calm despite the fact that he had been getting more and more beside himself at being kept waiting.

"Peters," said the captain, "we're taking Sanderson back to the states."

"Yes, sir," said Peters.

Sanderson, who had been staring vacantly at the proceedings in the cabin, began muttering again when his name was mentioned.

"I want you to make him comfortable," the captain continued.

"All right, sir," said Peters.

"I am Rawkaw the Mighty," intoned the madman. "I am the great medicine man of my people. I must not leave them to the evil spirits."

"Come on," said Peters, starting to seize the trader roughly by the shoulder.

"Peters, I said I wanted you to make him comfortable. I don't mean that I wanted you to manhandle him," said the captain. "He is a guest on this ship, and you've done enough to make the guests on this ship uncomfortable already." He looked significantly at Pieface.

For the moment Peters could not control his tongue. "You mean that I—?"

"I mean that you are to remember that I am skipper, and that I will not stand for any more monkey business," the captain interrupted. "Whatever suspicions I may have about things that have happened I keep to myself, but from now on you watch your step or there will be a new mate aboard this

vessel. Now take Sanderson away and
make him comfortable, and remember that
he is my guest, and all my guests are to be
treated as such. That's all."

Peters choked back the reply that was on
his lips. "Come on," he said to the trader.

"I am Rawkaw the Mighty, and I must
not leave my people to the evil spirits, said
the madman again.

Peters seemed to hear him for the first
time.

"Sure. Everything will be all right," he
said, taking the trader's arm affectionately
and leading him away.

"That's better, Peters," said the captain,
approvingly, as they went out.

"Yes, sir," said Peters.

But as the door closed behind him he
seemed to grin to himself, and it was not a
pleasant grin.

"So you are Rawkaw the Mighty," he
said to Sanderson, simulating admiration
and interest.

"I am the great medicine man of my
people."

"Fine," said Peters. "Come with me."

CHAPTER XVIII

PIEFACE PROVES USEFUL

THE situation at the trading post, with the trader unfitted for duty, presented a problem to the captain. The Eskimos were badly in need of supplies, and they had a good store of pelts on hand to exchange for the needed articles. The Eskimos are not a forethinking people, however, and Captain Carlson knew that to turn over the entire store of supplies intended for this post to the Eskimos themselves would be disastrous to the Eskimos as well as unprofitable to his firm. A riot of prodigality would ensue, and when the provisions were gone the Eskimos would have to go destitute until the arrival of the steamer again the following summer.

There was no other trading post near enough at hand to serve these people, and Captain Carlson felt that his duty to his company, as well as his humanitarian in-

stincts, prompted him to find a way to keep
the post active. He determined, therefore,
to persuade some member of his crew to take
over the trader's duties, at least until a new
man could be sent from the States.

None of the sailors was eager for the job,
however, and several days passed before the
captain had finally induced one of the deck-
hands to undertake it. Promises of a sub-
stantial reward, together with word pictures
of the monarch-like life of a trader, finally
accomplished it, and then the work of stock-
ing up the post was undertaken.

Meanwhile several days had passed, during which a remarkable friendship seemed
to have sprung up between Plugugly Peters
and the crazed Sanderson. The unbalanced
trader followed the mate about the ship much
as Pieface was wont to follow Wilson, and
Peters, for the first time since any one
aboard the ship had known him, seemed to
be friendly and indulgent—though his attitude toward all the others on board remained
the same as before.

Naturally this strange affair was the
cause of much surprised discussion among
the crew.

"Good playmate for the old grouch," was the cook's verdict.

"The man's crazy all right or he wouldn't have anything to do with Plugugly," opined the chief engineer.

"I don't care so much about goin' crazy," said the deck-hand who was to replace the trader, "but I hate to think that I might fall so low as to associate with Plugugly Peters through takin' this job."

Bill Johnson found less cause for joking in the friendship of the mate and the madman. "I don't like to be overly suspicious," he confided to Wilson, "but when that feller Plugugly starts gettin' chummy with anybody, crazy or not, there must be something behind it. I don't know what he's got in his mind, but I'll bet dollars to doughnuts he aims to use that poor feller some way or another. I'm goin' to keep my eyes open anyhow."

"I don't believe there's anything to get alarmed about," Wilson said. "What harm could that poor old idiot do to anybody even if Peters tried to stir him up to it. You're getting morbid, Bill."

"Maybe," said Bill. "Still I'll keep my eyes open."

"While you're keeping them open, I'm going down and see how Pieface is feeling," Wilson replied.

Pieface was still recuperating in the captain's cabin, and Wilson went there and knocked on the door. Bidden to enter, he found Captain Carlson writing at his table.

"May I see the patient?" he asked.

"Help yourself," said the captain. "I guess he'll be glad to entertain a visitor.

Pieface demonstrated the correctness of the captain's guess by standing up in his bed and barking a vociferous welcome.

"Sounds pretty healthy, doesn't he?" said the captain, over his shoulder. "I doubt if I can keep him in here much longer."

"Well, we must have him in condition for the trip south," said Wilson. He turned to the dog, "Mustn't we, old boy?"

Pieface wagged his tail, and stuck his head up to be patted. The life of an invalid bored him, even though it brought him the treatment of a favorite child. He craved action. He tried to show Wilson that he was feeling fit once more, in order that he might be allowed to follow him about the ship again, but his attempts irritated his wounds, and he sank back in his cushions with a sigh.

Wilson sat down beside him and stroked his head. "Guess you aren't quite well yet, are you, old boy?" he said. "Guess you'll have to stay in the hospital a little longer before you go out looking for another husky."

Another knock on the door interrupted Wilson's monologue.

"Come in," called the captain.

It was Peters.

"Mr. Sanderson wants to know if he can see you, sir," he said to the captain. "He's been begging to see you all day, and I've tried to get it off his mind, but I can't seem to do anything with him. I thought maybe if you'd just see him it might quiet him down."

"All right, Peters," said the captain. "What does he want to see me about?"

"Why you see, sir, he can't seem to get it out of his head that he is a medicine man, and that the Eskimos—his people, he calls 'em—will be destroyed by evil spirits or something if he leaves 'em."

"Yes, I know all about that," said the captain, "but what does he want me to do about it?"

"Why, he thinks you ought to let him stay here," the mate explained.

"But I can't do that. You know that, Peters."

"Yes, sir, I know it. And, as a matter of fact, I've been tryin' to tell Sanderson so, but it don't seem to do no good. So I thought maybe if you'd just see him—"

"Oh, very well, Peters. Send him in."

Peters hastened to carry the news to his friend the madman, and Wilson, feeling that he should not be in the captain's way, gave Pieface a final pat and went on deck. Pieface settled down for a nap, thinking that nothing more of interest was likely to happen for a while, now that Wilson's visit was over. He was snoring peacefully when Sanderson's timid rap came at the door.

Sanderson, as the captain well knew, had no new arguments to offer. But the captain decided to listen to him, and attempt again to reason with him. If this proved futile, as it probably would, he would be none the worse off for the interview, at least.

"Well, Sanderson," he said, "has Peters made you quite comfortable?"

"I am Rawkaw the Mighty. I am no longer Sanderson," pronounced the madman. "You must free me, that I may go back to my people and release them from the spell of the evil spirits."

"My dear Sanderson, you know that to be quite impossible," said the captain, trying to appear as though he were discussing an important deal with a perfectly normal man. "It is essential that you return at once to your people in the south. I would be neglecting my duty if I failed to bring you back to them."

"Rawkaw the Mighty has no people in the south. My people are here." He waved a hand in the general direction of the mainland.

"But John Sanderson has people in the south," argued the captain, "and you are John Sanderson."

"I am Rawkaw the Mighty," the madman persisted, parrot-like.

Argument, the captain perceived, was useless. "I'm very sorry, Sanderson," he said, finally, "but I cannot alter my plans. You must return to the States with us."

"That is final?" asked the madman, his eyes glittering with a weird light.

"That is final," the captain repeated. "I'm sorry, Sanderson."

"May I write a final note to my people?"

"Certainly, Sanderson."

"Will you give me a piece of paper?"

"Yes, indeed." The captain turned to a drawer of his table to produce the required paper.

As he turned his back, Sanderson whipped a knife from his shirt. Stealthily he crept closer, grinning sardonically as he paused for a moment behind the captain. Then he slowly lifted the knife over his head, and his lips formed the word "Raw-kaw."

Pieface had been awakened from his nap by the conversation between Sanderson and the captain. Although Sanderson had been in the cabin when the dog was brought there by Wilson several days before, he had been too much occupied by pain and weariness to pay any attention to him at that time. It was as though he saw him for the first time now, as he opened his eyes, and he was struck by the appearance of the man. Some instinct told him that this man was different from other men, and the man's actions and appearances seemed to bear out this feeling. Pieface half rose in his bed to study the man more attentively.

And now, as he looked, he saw the captain turn away from the man, and the man produce a knife from his shirt. Pieface stood up and stiffened, sensing trouble. Then he saw the man creep up behind the captain. He crouched and stiffened. Slowly the man's hand, clutching the knife, rose over his head.

Pieface waited no longer. Simultaneously he uttered a short, sharp yelp of warning to the captain, and sprang. Forgotten were his wounds, as he leaped to the rescue of his protector and friend. One thought only dominated his mind. He must strike before the knife descended.

He landed squarely on Sanderson's back, just as the knife fell. But the bark of warning had been enough to attract the captain's attention, and he dodged. Even this would have not have been enough, how-

ever, if the impact of the dog on Sanderson's back had not upset the madman's aim.
He swerved slightly in one direction, and
the captain dodged in the other. The knife
just grazed the captain's coat.

Pieface, having saved the captain from
death, was not yet content. This man was
an enemy, and the dog intended to settle
with him. Slipping down from Sanderson's
back after his first and effective lunge, he
crouched and sprang again, snapping at
Sanderson's throat with his teeth. Sanderson jumped, with a cry of fear, and Pieface missed his hold. The captain leaped
up.

"No, Pieface, no," he commanded,
"Steady now. It's all right."

Pieface, though disappointed, reluctantly
obeyed, and stood panting, ready to spring
into action again at a moment's notice. The
captain, fixing the now thoroughly terrified
Sanderson with his gaze, stretched out a
hand to Pieface's head.

"Good boy," he said. "Good boy."

It was praise enough, and Pieface was
happy.

CHAPTER XIX

JUSTICE IS DONE

"SANDERSON," said the captain, "give me that knife."

The madman, thoroughly cowed, did as ordered, blubbering like a baby. "I had to do it. I had to do it," he cried. "It was for my people."

"Sit down," said Captain Carlson, calmly. "Now, then, where did you get this knife?"

"He gave it to me," the madman wailed. "He understands. Only he understands. He knows that I am Rawkaw. He knows that I must stay with my people. He understands."

"He?" said the captain. "Who is he?"

"Oh I forgot. I must not tell. He said he would let me stay, but if I failed he would kill me. Oh, let me go. Please let me go."

"Come, come, Sanderson," said the captain, soothingly, "you are not going to be killed. But you must tell me what all this means."

He turned the knife over in his hands
several times, inspecting it reflectively, then
his countenance became firm and he looked
full at Sanderson. The madman flinched,
as though the captain's eyes were boring into
his very soul.

"Who gave you this knife?" the captain
demanded, enunciating each word slowly
and distinctly.

"Oh, he—he—oh, I can't."

"Who gave you this knife, Sanderson?"

The madman sank his head in his hands,
trying to hide from the captain's piercing
eyes. Tears of terror rolled out from between his clenched fingers. "No, no," he
wailed. "I can't. He'll kill me."

"Who gave you this knife?"

"Peters, Peters. Oh, where is he? Peters,
Peters, Peters." Sanderson's words trailed
off into an indistinct cry.

The captain set his jaw firmly. Pieface,
who had been watching the drama with tense
excitement, was unable to control himself
longer, and he lifted his head and barked
hoarsely, making a raucous chorus with the
madman's shrill wails. He became quiet

when the captain stretched out his hand and patted him.

Going to the door, the captain held it open and signalled to Pieface. "Go find Wilson," he ordered.

Pieface understood the command, and trotted away to obey it. Wilson was so surprised to see Pieface running around the vessel again that for the moment he thought the dog's attempts to lead him to the captain's cabin were mere antics, in exuberance of spirits. Presently, however, he perceived that Pieface was running always in one direction, apparently trying to get him to follow, and finally he did follow. Pieface led him straight to the cabin, where Captain Carlson bade him enter.

"Wilson," said the captain, "there is an ugly situation here. Sanderson just tried to stab me in the back, and would have done it if Pieface had not been too quick for him."

Wilson gasped in amazement, and Sanderson, his head still sunk in his hands, continued to mutter and sob incoherently.

"Of course Sanderson is not to be blamed," continued the captain. "The job was planned for him."

"Planned for him?" Wilson repeated, too horrified to say more.

"Yes," said the captain, as calmly as though he were talking of an everyday event. "It seems that Mr. Peters wanted to command the ship."

"Peters? Peters planned it?"

"Yes," said the captain.

"He was so good to me; and now he'll kill me," moaned the mad trader.

"Wilson," said the captain, "take Sanderson to Bill Johnson and tell him to look out for him. Then find Peters and send him to me at once."

"Yes, sir," said Wilson. "Come, Mr. Sanderson."

Sanderson followed meekly enough, and behind him trotted Pieface, acting as convoy and ready to pounce again at the slightest hint of trouble. His watchfulness was unnecessary, however, as Sanderson had no thought of further violence. Wilson took him to Bill, and in a few words told him what had happened. Then he went in search of the mate. Pieface hung at his heels.

Wilson found Plugugly on the after deck, standing alone and staring morosely into the

water. He was waiting for a message which
he knew must soon come, telling him either
that his plan had succeeded or that it had
failed. If it succeeded he would be in command of the steamer. If it failed——. He
hesitated to think of the consequences. Of
course there was a bare possibility that the
crazed trader might keep his mouth shut if
he failed to kill the captain. Perhaps his
mind was so thoroughly occupied with his
hallucinations that he would forget who had
prompted him to attempt murder. Plugugly
fervently hoped this would be the case—if
the plot failed. But the probability, he
knew, was that failure would mean exposure.
And nautical justice is firm. He shuddered.

Looking up he saw Wilson, and something about the youth's appearance told him
that the worst had happened. Sanderson
had failed, and he was exposed. He knew
it before a word had been spoken. Wilson's
words confirmed it.

"The captain wants you in his cabin at
once."

"What for?" snarled the mate, so filled
with fury and terror that he forgot that Wilson was only a subordinate carrying a mes-

sage from the captain to the second in command.

"He wants to see you, I suppose," said Wilson.

"You suppose he does, do you? Who are you to suppose?"

"He said 'at once'," said Wilson.

"Oh, he did, did he?" Plugugly snarled again. "And you're undertakin' to tell me to hurry, are you? Well, I'll go when I get good and ready, and I'll take no guff from you, see?"

Wilson, feeling that he had accomplished his mission, turned without further words and started to return to the cabin.

"Where you goin'?" Plugugly demanded.

"To the captain's cabin."

With a string of oaths, Plugugly lunged forward. "Not yet, you ain't," he shouted, and he seized Wilson by the coat collar.

"Let go," Wilson demanded.

Plugugly swore in reply, clung the harder, and with his free hand landed a blow on Wilson's jaw.

Ripping himself free, Wilson brought his own fists into play. A short month before he would have been as helpless in such an

encounter as a small child, but his life on the
sea had developed his body as well as his
mind, and the potential strength which his
physique had suggested had been converted
into actual strength in a remarkably short
time. He had also gained confidence in himself, and knew his own strength, so that the
prospects of a hand-to-hand battle with the
burly mate did not frighten him.

He swung right and left, and felt the
fierce joy of landing numerous resounding
blows on various parts of his adversary's
anatomy. His fists ached under such treatment, but the knowledge that they were
aching because of the force with which they
collided with Plugugly's jaw or ear or chest
made the ache almost pleasant.

But Plugugly was also getting in his full
quota of blows, and with the force of unpent
hate behind them. At first he punctuated
his blows with fierce, foul oaths, but after a
little while he began to feel the need of con-
serving his strength, and he fought silently,
as did Wilson.

There was little of pugilistic technique in
the battle, both Wilson and Plugugly
fighting almost blindly, but with all their

strength. Each, for the moment, had become primitive in his instincts, and it
mattered little how many blows were received, so long as others were given. They
fought on, blow for blow, panting and gasping for wind, but uttering no other sound
except an occasional involuntary grunt or
groan of pain.

It was settling down into a fight to ex-
haustion, and in such a fight it seemed inevitable that Plugugly, toughened by years
of the rugged seafaring life, must have the
advantage over the younger and less hardened Wilson. Yet Wilson was fighting not
only in self-defence, but also in rage against
the man who had shown himself to be a
murderous traitor as well as an unfeeling
brute, and he told himself grimly that
nothing less than the loss of consciousness
would serve to stop him.

The fight had gone on so firecely that
neither combatant had noticed the efforts of
Pieface to enter the fray. Yet he had been
trying. From the moment Plugugly had
attacked Wilson, he had been circling about,
looking for a chance to take Wilson's part.
Several times he had leaped at the mate,

only to miss his mark as the battlers swerved this way or that. Once he had managed to set his teeth into Plugugly's ankle, but the mate had hardly noticed him, so intent was he in the fight, and the dog had soon lost his grip, which had been none too firm in the first place.

Finally, however, he got a firm hold on the fleshy part of Plugugly's calf, and this time he sank his teeth so deep that the mate cried out in pain. Whirling about, Peters drew back his free leg to launch a kick at the clinging terrier. As he did so, he left himself temporarily unguarded from Wilson's swinging blows. Wilson saw his opportunity. He mustered every last ounce of strength, and swung full at Plugugly's jaw. The mate, unprepared for the blow, and half off his balance anyway because of his kick at the dog, staggered and fell heavily to the deck.

Wilson knew that this was no time for etiquette. He knew that if the situation were reversed, his own chances of ever rising again would be slight. Peters, he knew, would have taken full advantage of having his adversary down. As for himself, he had no desire to carry the affair to any brutal lengths, but neither did he intend that the advantage should be lost. Without hesitation, therefore, he leaped astride the fallen mate, and pinned him to the deck.

Pieface, feeling that he should have a share of the fruits of a victory in which he had been a vital factor, also sprang at the mate, and would have inflicted serious punishment if Wilson had not ordered him to desist. He obeyed the order sadly. It seemed that he was never to be allowed to finish anything he started.

It was remarkable that the fight had gone as long as it had without attracting attention. It was only as the telling blow was struck, however, that any of the members of the crew happened to be near enough to hear the commotion. Once the fight was discovered it was a matter of seconds before the crowd began to gather.

Wilson was well satisfied to be discovered. He had intended to hold Plugugly to the deck until somebody came, and here came a crowd almost as he thought of it.

A great shout went up as the men saw Wilson astride the hated mate. Wilson disheveled and gasping for breath, paid little heed to the admiring exclamations of his shipmates. Peters had already started to try to squirm out of his clutches, but had desisted when the men began to gather, knowing that they would prevent a resumption of the fight. Wilson leaned close to his ear.

"Are you going to the captain?" he asked in a low voice.

Plugugly grunted a baleful assent.

Wilson started to rise. As he did so, however, there was a rustle among the sailors, and Captain Carlson pushed his way through them. He paused in astonishment as he saw the cause of the commotion.

"What's this?" he demanded.

Wilson stood up. "I'm sorry, sir," he said. "He attacked me when I told him you wanted to see him, and we fought."

The captain looked scornfully at the still recumbent figure of his mate. "I should say you did," he said.

"He would have beaten me but for Pieface," Wilson admitted.

"Pieface took a hand, too, did he?" said

the captain. "He's mixing up in quite a few affairs lately, isn't he?"

He laid his hand on Wilson's shoulder, reaching down with the other to scratch the attentive terrier on the ear. "Well," he said, "I'm sorry you beat Peters up—in a way. I wanted to do it myself. Should have, by rights. The skipper should do his own beating, I believe, but still you've done a pretty good job of it, so we'll let it go at that. You and Pieface did my job for me, that's all."

He turned to the gaping sailors. "Peters is no longer the mate of this vessel," he said.

The men almost cheered, but caught themselves, suddenly realizing that something more serious than this fight must have occurred to bring about such an announcement. Yet the next announcement was even more breath-taking.

"He is under arrest for the remainder of the voyage. You men take him below and put him in irons."

Never was a task undertaken with a more willing spirit.

"Not too rough," the captain had to caution them. "Remember he just got a good beating."

"Wilson, my lad," he said, "bring Pie-face down to my cabin."

CHAPTER XX

HEADING FOR HOME

PIEFACE was now doubly a hero. He had saved the captain's life, and he had helped to trounce the villainous mate. Nothing was too good for him after these two exploits. Previously he had been accorded favoritism. Now he was accorded honor.

The wounds left by his battle with the husky soon healed, and once more he resumed his custom of strolling majestically over the vessel, holding his head proudly, breathing the sea air deep into his lungs and only pausing in his progress when he came upon one of the select few whom he deigned to consider worthy of more than a casual friendship. His was not the pride of accomplishment, however, for he gave himself much less credit for his recent activities than did his associates. His, rather, was a natural pride, born of good canine blood and fostered by the virile, soul-satisfying life into which Wilson had inadvertently brought him. He took a keen joy in living, and one who does that, man or dog, seldom is dissatisfied with himself.

Captain Carlson, who had been drawn to the dog from the first, was naturally even more beneficent to him now that he owed him his very life.

"I've a mind to make Pieface mate in Peters's place," he said smilingly, as he and Wilson and the terrier were doing a turn about the deck. "At least he's a good dog, and that's more than can be said for Peters."

The remark showed what was on the captain's mind. With Peters languishing in irons below decks, and with everything in readiness for the start south, something had to be done about filling the post left vacant by Plugugly's forced retirement.

"If you were just a bit older Wilson and had a little more experience aboard ship, blamed if I wouldn't rather have you for a mate than most anybody I can think of," continued the captain, more seriously.

Wilson tried to smile, but succeeded only

in achieving an embarrassed blush. "You've been very kind to me," he said.

The captain waved a deprecating hand. "You've earned all you've got," he said, almost gruffly. "But on second thought, I wouldn't have you for a mate. You're too good material for an ordinary seafaring man."

He fell silent, and Wilson, feeling very much embarrassed by such high praise, studied the deck.

"I tell you what to do, Wilson," said the captain, finally. "You run and find your fisherman friend, Bill Johnson, and send him to me. I'll be down in my cabin."

"Yes, sir," said Wilson.

This, he decided, meant that the captain had chosen Bill as the successor to Plugugly. It pleased him immensely. Having passed most of his life on fishing boats, Bill had had little difficulty in acclimating himself to life on a trading steamer, and had soon become one of the most efficient members of the crew. It was good to see his abilities recognized.

He hastened to find Bill, and without giving him any hint of the thoughts running through his brain, merely told him that the captain wanted to see him. Bill answered the summons with his usual good humor, ex-· pecting to be assigned to some routine duty or other. He emerged from the cabin, how- ever, with a glint of happiness in his eyes, and quickly sought out Wilson to tell him the big news.

"The old man wants me to ship as mate for the rest of the voyage," he said.

"I had an idea that was what he wanted," Wilson replied.

"You did?" Bill repeated, looking at his friend with a sort of wondering admiration. "You was way ahead o'me, wa'nt you?"

Captain Carlson immediately announced his new appointment, and at the same time gave orders for sailing. The steamer was now to proceed south again, stopping at the various other trading posts en route. The unexpected delay of the last few days meant that no more time must be lost, and the preparations for departure went ahead with dispatch.

During the next few weeks life on ship- board was calm. Plugugly was safely be- low, where he could do no harm; Sanderson, having been taken out of sight of his old trading post, fell into an imbecillic indolence; Bill Johnson settled into the duties of the mate as though he had never done anything else; all was serene.

The ship visited half a dozen trading posts, leaving supplies and taking on furs and such other articles as had been gathered in by the traders. Steadily she pushed on toward home, and the men began to talk of waiting wives, children, mothers, or sweethearts.

Wilson alone, of all the crew, looked forward to the homecoming with no pleasure. He no longer flinched to think of the contempt in which his former fair-weather friends would now hold him. Instead he felt a touch of contempt for them. The old life of idleness held no lure for him longer; he had tasted the sweeter fruits of an active, self-sufficient life. The only face that he would have taken pleasure in seeing again was that of the formerly despised Joe Kirkup, and realizing the baseness of his conduct a few short weeks before he felt ashamed, and was glad that the steamer was not going to put in at Miquelon. He would

send Joe a telegram telling him that he and
Pieface were all right, he decided.

Wives, mothers, sweethearts—these were
what the other men were talking about. But
Pieface was all these in one to Wilson, and
Pieface was with him. And it was only
aboard ship that this close friendship had
been welded. Who knew what would happen once they were on shore again? There
seemed to be something about the atmosphere at sea that made for contentment. In
this atmosphere Pieface had forgiven him his
cruelty and in this atmosphere he had re-
pented that cruelty. There seemed to be
something almost mystical about it, and
Wilson, musing, wondered if all his contentment would fade when he stepped on dry
land again. He pictured Pieface suddenly
turning on him.

These gloomy thoughts were reflected on
his face as he stood staring morosely into
the water. He was so absorbed that he did
not hear Pieface come up behind him, followed at a little distance by Captain Carlson. The dog, sensing the austerity of Wilson's mood, planted himself at the youth's
side, cocking his head upward, and stood

in respectful silence. Captain Carlson also stood still for a few minutes wondering at Wilson's solemn preoccupation.

Then the captain moved up to the rail beside him, and placed a companionable hand on his shoulder. Wilson jumped, startled, then smiled feebly to hide his con‹ fusion.

"You look as though you were just about to jump overboard," said the captain jovially, but with frank curiosity.

"Oh, no," said Wilson, "I was just thinking."

"About the future?" asked the captain.

Wilson showed his surprise that the captain should divine his thoughts. "Why, yes—in a way," he confirmed.

"Got any plans?"

"No—that is, I'd like to keep on sailing with you if you'd have me—and Pieface."

"Have you?" repeated the captain. "My boy, for my part nothing would please me better than to have you stay with me. And as for the old sea dog, I don't know what the ship will be without him."

"But you aren't going to keep us?" cried Wilson, noting the negative implication of the captain's words. "Please do. I could learn a lot more, and I would work hard."

"Not a doubt of it. Not a doubt of it," said the captain. "But that's not the point. There's no question but that you would be well worth your pay as a member of any ship's crew, and far as I'm concerned I'd sign you up if you couldn't do a thing, just for the sake of having you and Pieface along for company. But that's not the point."

"Then what is the point, sir?" asked Wilson, hoping to be able to advance an argument to meet whatever objection was in the captain's mind.

"The point is, as I've told you before, that you're too good material for this sort of a life. You've got the stuff to amount to something in the world, more than being an ordinary old salt like Bill Johnson and me."

"But I like it," Wilson protested. "I want to do it. I'd rather do it than anything else."

"You're young, Wilson," said the captain, "and you've never tried anything else that was worth while. But there are other things."

Abruptly he seemed to change the subject. "Have you any friends or relatives to go to when we get back to port?" he asked.

Wilson shook his head gloomily.

"Well, I'll tell you what," said the captain. "We're heading for Boston, as you know, and over in Charlestown, not too far from the waterfront, I've got a trim little house and a trim little wife. But that's all— no youngsters and no dogs. Now what I suggest is that you just come along with me—you and Pieface—and we'll just have a gay old homecoming. And you just wait until you try the doughnuts we'll have."

"You're very kind," said Wilson. "I should like to very much."

"Fine," said the captain. "And as for Pieface, here, we'll provide such a banquet of bones for him that he'll be as stuffed as a Thanksgiving turkey."

Pieface, as usual, responded to the sound of his name by a bark. The captain, beaming, gave him a careless pat on the head and walked away.

"Think of the doughnuts and cheer up," he called back over his shoulder.

"I will," Wilson replied.

But he was still far from cheerful in appearance after the captain had disappeared from sight. He leaned against the rail and ran his fingers over Pieface's back and head. The dog seemed so thoroughly at home on shipboard that Wilson found it difficult to picture him happy anywhere else—even at a bone feast in Captain Carlson's house.

"Well, seadog," he said, "we've got to learn to be landlubbers, you and I."

Pieface barked again, joyfully.

"If you knew what I was talking about, I'll bet you wouldn't be so happy about it," said Wilson.

But Pieface did not know, and again he barked, joyfully.

"Oh, well," said Wilson, "let's make the most of it while we're here." And he rolled Pieface over on his back, then ran down the deck, temptingly. Pieface jumped up and gave chase.

He loved the gentle rolling of the steamer under his feet.

CHAPTER XXI

CATASTROPHE

THE last trading post had been visited; the summer was nearly gone, and the "Sturdy" was on the home stretch. Down below decks Plugugly Peters still writhed in irons, while elsewhere on the ship the men sang about their work. The voyage was nearly over.

Even Pieface realized that something unusually pleasant was in the air, though it is doubtful if he would have considered it pleasant had he known that the vague "something" was the end of a voyage which he had found in every way delightful. It troubled him somewhat to see that Wilson did not seem to enter whole-heartedly into the new spirit of the ship, and out of sympathy he sometimes grew slightly doleful himself, trying to discourage an outburst of levity on the part of some of the other members of the crew; but most of the

time he found the gay spirit too much to
his liking to be resisted, and was unusually
playful even with those whom he usually
ignored.

But there came a day when the light spirit
aboard the steamer was submerged. Storm
clouds brewed—unusually severe storm
clouds for the time of year, and every mind
was given over to thoughts of weathering
the approaching storm. In this exigency
Bill Johnson, as mate, became a veritable
human dynamo, and Captain Carlson was
here, there, and everywhere, looking after
all the details to which attention had to be
given.

The Nova Scotian coast had been left behind, and the steamer was proceeding along
the rugged coast of northern Maine. But
as the storm clouds thickened, the coast line
became less and less distinct, and presently
it was lost to sight entirely. The seas
chopped and pounded with increasing fury,
and the little steamer wallowed in the churning waters like a bobbin in a mill pond.
Gamely she fought her way onward, but at
times she seemed to be butting her prow

against a stone wall, so fiercely did the great waves oppose her.

With nightfall the storm seemed to increase in fury. Rain scudded down in sheets, and the steamer's lights seemed like puny candles trying to pierce the darkness. The steady chug-chug of the engine was almost drowned out by the screaming of the wind and the creaking of the struggling vessel. Still she buffeted her way along.

It was Pieface's first experience in a storm of any consequence, and his excitement was unbounded. As the storm had come on, converting the gentle rolling of the ship, which he loved, into a wild, unsteady lurching, he had been angry and amazed. Finding that barking failed to have any effect, however, and sensing the excitement of his shipmates, he had given himself over to a like reaction. Running here and there, barking and growling, he had been as busy as the busiest of men, and had there been time for amusement his attempts to participate in the general activities would have been highly appreciated. Since the men were all too busy to be amused, they let him run and bark and growl at first, until he had

barely escaped being washed overboard
several times, after which Bill Johnson
picked him up bodily and carried him below,
shutting him up in the cabin for safe-keep-
ing. There he remained, horribly unhappy
at being shut up away from the scene of
activity; frankly frightened, now that he was
alone, of the violent motion of the ship in
the storm; eager to get out again and help
in the struggle against the storm by his running and barking and growling. All night
long he waited for his release, too excited
to sleep.

But this was an emergency in which the
gallant terrier could not play the rôle of
hero. This was a battle against nature, and
a dog's teeth, sharp and strong as they might
be, could not serve.

It was a battle against nature, but nature,
Captain Carlson feared, had an ally. He
confided his fears to his new mate.

"I'm not just comfortable about the compass," he said. "It's seemed a little off in
the last day or two, though perhaps I am
just getting worrisome in my old age. Still
I don't like the thought of it in this storm."

" 'Twould be a bad time for the compass

to get finicky, that's a fact," Bill agreed. "Still I guess we'll get through all right."

"Oh, of course," said the captain, hastily, half ashamed of his fears. "Just thought I'd mention it to you so you could take all the precautions possible. This is a real storm for this time of year, eh?"

"Sure is," said Bill, and the conference ended.

The night wore on, with the ship plugging away doggedly in the face of the storm. Everything having been done which it was possible to do, except for keeping a strict watch, Bill Johnson sent most of the men below to get some sleep. Wilson was among them. He protested against Bill's orders, feeling himself privileged by his friendship with the acting mate, but Bill was firm.

Going below, Wilson found Pieface wide-eyed and ready for action. The dog barked eagerly when he saw Wilson, but lapsed into a low whine when he saw that this arrival did not mean his release. He still refused to sleep, even when Wilson turned into his bunk and closed his eyes.

Wilson dropped off to sleep and although as a matter of fact he had been asleep several hours it seemed only a moment later when the steamer suddenly trembled all over like a shack in an earthquake, and then, with a grinding, grating sound, bumped violently to a halt.

Men tumbled out of their bunks with cries of startled inquiry and alarm. From above came a stentorian yell, "All hands on deck." But even before the yell was completed, the order was being obeyed. Struggling into jackets as they ran, the men hurried above.

"What is it? What's happened?" Wilson asked the man nearest him.

"We're aground. That's what," was the reply. "We'll be lucky to get out of it in this storm, too, if you ask me."

All around him Wilson heard similar sentiments being expressed. As he ran on deck he heard Captain Carlson's voice above all the tumult, issuing orders, calm, unafraid, but piercing and unmistakable. Now and then Bill's voice broke in. Men scurried to and fro.

Bill was supervising the placing of the signal lights, while the captain sent the engineer and firemen below with orders for a fresh attempt to get the ship clear. Wilson helped with the lights, and Pieface, released at last, ran after him, barking furiously in uncontrollable excitement.

The attempt to get clear failed, as the captain had expected it would. The ship trembled and groaned in travail, but it budged not an inch forward or back. Yet it teetered and staggered under the wild pounding of the surf, dipping every now and then to meet a great white-cap, shivering as if in cold as the wave broke and the water rolled over the deck, then righting itself again, ready for a fresh attack.

"It's no use. We're fast," called the captain to Bill. "Let go with the signal rockets."

In a moment the rockets were sending aloft their fiery message of distress. Wilson, who before had always thought of rockets as a means of celebration, was impressed with the fact that they could send forth such a weird and awe-inspiring light when used in an utterly serious business. But to Pieface they were merely rockets—and rockets at any time were most exciting things. For the moment he forgot to be frightened at the unusual motion of the ship, so intense was the pleasurable excitement he derived from the flying fire.

As the rockets blazed, the men on the ship could make out the shore line, only about a hundred and twenty-five feet away. But between the stranded ship and the shore was such a torrent of raging water that there could be no thought of crossing it. And meanwhile the waves pounded, pounded, pounded. The little steamer, already well battered by years, could not hold together long under such a lashing.

"What if our signals are not seen?" Wilson asked Bill, as the latter paused a moment by his side.

"Then we wait for the storm to pass," said the mate.

"But the ship? Will it stand it?"

Bill shrugged. "Guess the signals will be seen," he said. "If I remember aright, there's a coast-guard station just down the coast."

Yet the long minutes lengthened into an hour, and the sky began to light up, and still the angry waves lashed the helpless ship. Then, in the vague half-light of dawn.

somebody espied moving figures on the shore. Quickly the word passed around, and a great cry went up. It was the coast guard.

In the dim dawn light the anxious men aboard the steamer watched their rescuers preparing to save them. They were rigging up a breeches buoy, and Captain Carlson waved with his hands to signify that those on the steamer were ready to make the end of the apparatus fast, once it had been shot aboard from the cannon which was being made ready for the purpose on the shore.

Finally the guardsmen were ready, and the precious line came hurtling aboard the steamer. Eager hands seized it, and pulled after it the stronger cable to which it was attached. This they made fast, while the guardsmen attended to their end. Then the carrier was propelled from the shore, over the cable, to the ship for the first passenger.

Captain Carlson was about to single Wilson out as the first to go ashore, but as he called to the youth Bill Johnson spoke into his ear. A shocked expression came over the captain's face.

"I'd entirely forgotten," he exclaimed. "He's still in irons. He must be released at once."

"Peters?" asked Wilson, overhearing the words as he answered the captain's beckoning sign. "I'll go below and release him, sir."

"No, no," said the captain. "You're going ashore."

But already somebody else had taken advantage of Wilson's delay and the captain's lack of attention to climb into the breeches, and even as the captain spoke the carrier went sliding shoreward.

"Well, all right," said captain. "Here's the key. You'll have to be quick about it."

Wilson ran below, where Plugugly, thinking he had been entirely forgotten or purposely left to perish, was nearly fainting with fear. He babbled incoherent cries for help and mercy, as Wilson ran toward him. Wilson wasted no words, but unlocked his shackles and urged him to hurry on deck.

Peters, weakened and unnerved by his long confinement, tried to obey these instructions, but his knees sank under him as he stepped, and he fell helplessly at Wilson's feet. Wilson lifted him up, and exerting all his strength, half dragged and half carried him up to the deck.

Half the men already were ashore by the time this task was accomplished. Those who remained ran to Wilson's assistance as soon as he got the helpless ex-mate in sight. Unanimously they accorded him the next turn in the breeches buoy, and as soon as it came aboard again they lifted him into it and sent him sliding ashore.

Wilson now bethought himself of Pieface and began looking around for the dog. He was nowhere to be seen.

"Where's Pieface?" he yelled into the ear of his nearest companion, shouting to make himself heard over the din of the pounding surf.

"Guess somebody must have took him ashore," the other shouted in reply, after a hasty glance around him.

Similar replies came from others whom Wilson asked, although nobody had actually seen the dog being taken ashore.

"You're next, Wilson," Captain Carlson shouted, as the buoy returned again.

"But Pieface? Where's Pieface?" Wilson asked.

"Somebody must have taken him," replied the captain. "Otherwise he'd be here."

Wilson took another desperate look around.

"He'll probably be waiting for you on shore," said the captain, reassuringly.

"If he isn't, I'm coming back," shouted Wilson, stepping into the breeches. Then he was riding above the whitecaps, and in a few minutes the coast guardsmen lifted him out of the carrier to the ground. The carrier was again sliding toward the ship.

"Did you see a dog?" Wilson asked the coast guardsmen.

"Dog? No, I didn't see him."

"Neither did I."

"Nor I."

Nobody had seen him. He was not ashore.

"I'm going back. I must go back," cried Wilson.

"Back where?" asked the astonished guardsman to whom he addressed himself.

"Back aboard the steamer. I must get my dog."

"Not much, you don't," said the guardsman. "We just took you off that steamer. Now you stay off."

"But my dog—I've got to save him."

"There, there, brother, don't take on like that," said the guardsman, surprised and softened by the display of such unselfish devotion to a dog. "If he's aboard, they'll bring him ashore."

"But he must be aboard, if he's not here," Wilson insisted, pleadingly. "And they won't bring him because he must be hiding somewhere. I looked around before I came ashore and he wasn't in sight."

"He'll likely show up before the last of 'em's come ashore," said the guardsman. Then he added soberly, "Or else he's been washed overboard."

Wilson caught his breath at this suggestion. For an instant his mind flashed back to the time when he had left Pieface struggling in the water off Miquelon. He shuddered as the picture came back to him.

"Oh, please let me go back. I must. I must," he pleaded.

"It's no use. If he's there, they'll bring him. Otherwise he's already overboard, and it's too late to do anything about it," said

the guardsman, shaking his head pityingly.
The other guardsmen shook their heads in
agreement.

One of them laid a companionable hand
on Wilson's shoulder. "Too bad, old man,"
he said.

"Tough luck," said another.

They were accustomed to the tragedies of
the sea, these men, but not hardened to
them, and they were really sorry, but being
convinced that it would be a fool's errand
for Wilson to return to the stranded
steamer, they held it their duty to deny his
plea.

One by one the remaining men were
brought to shore. Bill Johnson was next to
last, leaving only the captain. As Bill
landed Wilson rushed up to him.

"Pieface isn't here," he cried.

Bill looked quickly back toward the
steamer.

"He must have been washed overboard,"
he muttered.

Silently he and Wilson watched the captain climb into the breeches and slide
toward them. Then suddenly Wilson uttered a sharp cry.

"There he is. There he is," he shouted, pointing toward the ship.

Bill looked. The guardsmen looked. The captain, stepping to the ground, looked too, although he did not know what was causing the commotion. And as he stepped to the ground Wilson stepped into the breeches.

"I'm going back," he cried. "I'm going to get him."

The guardsmen looked at one another. Then, as though by previous agreement, they sent Wilson flying back toward the ship.

Pieface saw him coming. The dog had been looking for him ever since he went below to release Peters. It was in search of Wilson that Pieface had gone wandering around the boat, out of sight, nearly forfeiting his life by so doing. Now he had returned to the deck and found it deserted, but Wilson was riding toward him in some kind of a queer rigging. He ran to meet him, and Wilson, hardly stopping at all, picked him up, settled into his place again, and waved a signal to the men on shore.

Pieface barked, enjoying the novel ride.

CHAPTER XXII

PIEFACE MAKES A CHOICE

THE "Sturdy," true to its name, dog-gedly refused to go to pieces under the fierce battering of the storm, but when another sundown brought calmer weather the vessel was so weakened that its cargo had to be removed. A few days later the old "Sturdy" was towed into a nearby port and laid up for repairs. The crew was sent home, and Sanderson was sent to Boston in care of the chief engineer.

Captain Carlson, bemoaning the fact that the rugged little steamer would never be fit for another northern voyage, took Wilson and Pieface home with him for the promised feast. They said good-by to Bill Johnson in Portland, not, however, until after the captain had tried vainly to persuade the fisherman to ship again as his mate when he was ready for another voyage.

"Thank ye kindly," said Bill, "but I

don't see how I can come to it. I'm a fisherman, and the only reason I ever was anything else was because I lost hold of my
fisherman's luck for the time bein'. I'll get
it back again now, and when you're galli-
vantin' around up in Hudson Bay or some
other place, I'll be right to home on the
good old Banks."

No amount of argument would serve to
make him change his mind. So he gripped
Wilson's hand in one of his own, rubbed
Pieface's attentive head with the other, and
strode away. "I leave these two here to you
Cap'n," he said. "That ought to be enough."

Pieface, sensing that this departure was
more than a mere temporary separation,
made three or four hesitating steps in the
direction of the departing Bill. Then he
stopped and barked, inviting Bill to recon-
sider and return. But Bill only turned his
head and waved his hand, then disappeared
around a corner. Pieface hastened to rejoin
Wilson and the captain, lest he lose them
also.

They went on to Boston by train, much
to Pieface's disgust. Accustomed as he
was to the freedom of a ship and the exhil-

arating sea air, he found it extremely an-
noying to be shut up in a stuffy baggage
car, bumping along over steel tracks. It
seemed as though the trip would never end,
and he began to think that he was entering into a new manner of life—as disagreeable as the shipboard life had been agreeable. His throat, from which usually came
a full-souled bark, now sent forth a whine.
But he barked again with redoubled joy
when he was taken from the train in Boston
and trundled into a taxicab for the trip
across town to Captain Carlson's home. It
was a great relief to find that the train life
was not to be permanent.

There followed days devoted wholly to
the pursuit of happiness. Captain Carlson's
promises concerning feasts were more than
carried out by Mrs. Carlson, who made
Wilson and Pieface feel thoroughly at
home in her neat little house. They ate
and romped and made merry, with the
captain and Mrs. Carlson participating
fully in the merriment.

But there was something unreal about
it all to both of them. Wilson knew that
it could not last; he must find a means of

supporting himself soon; life must be faced. Pieface, taking full advantage of the opportunities provided him for eating, dozing, and romping, yet had a feeling that this was not normal. Normalcy, he felt, involved a ship and the sea. This was merely a temporary change, pleasant for a time, but not to be considered permanent. He had given up all idea of permanency in connection with life on land when the train ride came to its welcome end.

Then came a day when the captain asked Wilson to go for a walk with him. Pieface, of course, accompanied them. And as they walked the captain talked.

"The company is fitting out a new ship for me," he said, "and I'll be off on another voyage as soon as she's ready."

Wilson was silent, looking wistful.

"You still think you'd like to follow the sea?"

"Oh, yes, Captain," replied Wilson eagerly. "Have you changed your mind? Will you take Pieface and me with you?"

The captain shook his head. "No, I can't do it, Wilson," he said. "It wouldn't be right. I wish I could. But you've got bigger things ahead of you, and I want to help you instead of holding you back."

They walked on wordlessly for a time, finally reaching the shipyard where the captain's new ship was being fitted out. The captain exhibited it proudly, as a man might exhibit his favorite son to his friends. Wilson shared his enthusiasm, but it only made him the more sad to think that he could never become a part of this ship, as he had felt himself a part of the "Sturdy." Pieface, having no such realization, found the ship altogether delightful. Noticing the proprietary air with which the captain proceeded here and there, he assumed that he could make himself right at home, and did so. It was wonderful to be on a ship again, even though it were in a yard; it would be more wonderful, Pieface thought, to go voyaging again. He had no doubt that this would soon come to pass.

He would not have been so confident had he been able to understand what the captain was saying to Wilson as they walked home.

"I don't want to seem to take charge of your life, Wilson," he said, "but I should be very happy if you would let me make some suggestions and perhaps help you a little, here and there."

"Why, of course," said Wilson. "You have been very kind, and—"

"Tush, tush," the captain interrupted. "None of that now. Well, then, here is my suggestion. I happen to know that my company could use a bright young fellow in their office, and give him every chance to make something of himself. It seems to me that you are just the man for them. You have brains, education, and you have learned something of one end of the business already by going with me. Now, as a matter of fact, I have spoken about you to some of the big men up there, and if you want to try it, the job's yours."

Wilson stuttered, too astonished to be coherent, "Why, why—"

"Of course if you have something else in mind," said the captain, disappointed at what he thought to be Wilson's hesitation.

"No, no," said Wilson quickly. "Of course I would like it. You are so—"

Again the captain forestalled his outburst of gratitude. "Fine," he said. "Then that's settled. Now the next thing is where are you going to live?"

"Why, I will have to find a room somewhere, of course," said Wilson.

"Well, now," said the captain, "I tell you what I wish you would do. I wish you would stay right at my house. You see Mrs. Carlson and I never had any youngsters of our own, and it would be very nice to have somebody we could sort of look at as our boy. Then it would be better for Pieface, too, than living in a furnished room somewhere."

Wilson did not try to express his gratitude this time. It showed in his face.

"I—I thought may be you would like to take Pieface with you, even if I don't go," he said at last.

"So I would. So I would," said the captain quickly. "But I know how hard it would be for you to give him up, and I reckon he would be just as slow about giving you up. No, I guess Pieface and you will stick together."

"I'm not so sure he would prefer to stay with me," said Wilson. "He likes the sea more than almost anything. You can see that."

"Yes, he's all sea dog," the captain agreed. "But still I doubt it he would go if he were given his choice."

"Let's give him his choice, then, and let that decide it," Wilson suggested.

"Done," said the captain, and they shook hands on it.

"It's a sporting offer," the captain said. "I like you all the better for it."

They returned home, where Mrs. Carlson prepared an entirely new feast in honor of Wilson's acccptance of the captain's proposition.

The arrangements for Wilson's job were soon completed, and he began his new duties within a few days. Pieface fell into the habit of walking part way with him, then going down to the waterfront. Usually he found his way to the captain's new ship, and made himself thoroughly at home on it. It was the next best thing to sailing.

At last the ship was launched and all was in readiness for the captain's departure on a new voyage. Most of his old crew was aboard, though there was a new mate and one or two other new faces. Wilson and Pieface went aboard an hour before the ship was to sail. They joined the captain and Mrs. Carlson in the cabin after greeting their old shipmates.

Pieface was intensely happy. The ship was in the water; the captain was in his cabin; the crew was aboard; it could mean but one thing—sailing. He chose a comfortable corner and curled up in it, lost in pleasant anticipation.

Eventually he was brought out of his reverie by hearing his name called, and he roused himself and followed Captain and Mrs. Carlson and Wilson out of the cabin and up to the gangplank. The captain walked out to the middle of the gangplank, where he kissed his wife. She walked across to the dock. The captain and Wilson remained, with Pieface between them.

"Well, Wilson, good-by," said the captain, extending his hand.

"Good-by, Captain," said Wilson.

They studiously avoided looking at the dog, who watched the ceremony wonderingly.

Then, as though at a signal, both turned

and started to walk: the captain, toward the ship; Wilson, toward the dock. Pieface stood uncertainly in his tracks.

What could this mean? Was Wilson not going to sail? Pieface found it difficult to imagine such a probability. Yet Wilson was leaving and the captain was returning aboard the ship. He, Pieface, was left to follow the one or the other. Perhaps he was mistaken. Perhaps Wilson would return before the ship sailed. But if he did not—

To sail on a ship again! Pieface had thought he wanted to do that above all things. But now he was not so sure. Sailing on a ship without Wilson was something he had never imagined before. Perhaps Wilson would come back. Very well, if he did come back, Pieface would come back with him. But he could not leave Wilson.

He trotted across to the dock.

Wilson, hearing the dog behind him, turned and held out his hands. Pieface leaped up at him, and he hugged him violently. Pieface had chosen him over the sea. His happiness was beyond words.

"Good old Pieface. Good old Pieface."
It was all he could say.

Pieface licked his hands, then turned and
looked rather wistfully at the ship as the
gangplank was pulled up. Then they were
not going—he and Wilson. He was sorry.
He had wanted to go.

He turned again to Wilson. Perhaps he
could persuade him to change his mind yet.
He barked to get his master's attention,
then looked toward the steamer and barked
again, plaintively. Already the ship was
moving slowly away from the dock, but
Pieface, eagerness burning in his eyes, was
ready to jump into the water and pursue it,
if Wilson would only give a sign of consent.

But Wilson stood still and shook his
head.

"No, old boy, we can't go." he said.

Pieface morosely watched the ship, now
gaining headway as it moved into the harbor. For a moment he thought he would
be unable to keep himself from jumping
into the water and giving chase. It seemed
as though a very vital part of him was
sailing away with the captain's ship, and
that he could not live any more after the

ship had passed from sight. Wilson's voice, sympathetic and calm, stilled his wild fancy.

"No, old boy."

The ship was now well out in the harbor. In a little while it would pass out into the wider waters of the ocean, and they would see it no more. Pursuit would then be out of the question. But if only they could start now, perhaps they could catch it. Pieface looked at Wilson again, pleading.

"We can't go, old boy. We just can't."

Sadly Pieface turned his head away. And then a new sight took his attention. Down at the other end of the dock, also gazing out at the departing ship, was a man. He was slouched, unkempt, shabby. Yet there seemed to be something wistful about his appearance, too. Was the ship taking away a part of him also? Pieface wondered.

He looked more attentively, and something about the man seemed familiar. Unpleasantly familiar. Suddenly he knew, and with a low growl he turned and ran toward the lone watcher with all his speed, converting the growl into a series of sharp, antagonistic barks as he ran.

Wilson, intent on watching the ship,

turned in surprise as the dog started. He looked down the dock, in the direction in which Pieface was running. A man, evidently the object of Pieface's pursuit, was running, too, casting frightened looks over his shoulder as he ran. Then the man jumped aboard a passing truck, pulling himself up to safety, where the dog would be unable to reach him. From his safe perch he shook his fist and began shouting, cursing.

Then Wilson knew him. It was Plug-ugly Peters.

CHAPTER XXIII

FATES

A WISPY, merry crackling fire burned in the open fireplace of the Carlson home. In a huge armchair in front of it sat a young man. At his feet was a dog. Outside a chill wind hurled great snowflakes against the window panes.

The young man laid down the book he had been reading, and walked to the window.

"Aren't you glad you're not at sea today, Pieface?" he asked.

The dog, rather reluctantly, left his warm place on the hearth and joined his master. A short bark, which might have meant anything, was his only reply to the question. Then he focused his gaze on a picture on the wall—a picture of a ship at sea—and the longing expression in the dog's eyes answered Wilson's question better than words would have done.

Wilson returned to his chair by the fire, and picked up a newspaper. But for the moment he let it rest in his lap as he watched the flickering blaze dreamily. He could scarcely realize that he was Wilson Bersey—the same Wilson Bersey who used to trot idly about the Continent, despising tutors and others whom he considered beneath him in the social scale; the same Wilson Bersey who gave way to rage and despondency when fortune turned against him; the same Wilson Bersey who tried to drown a dog, this dog, the one and only Pieface; the same Wilson Bersey who had beseeched the skipper of a rum-runner to accept him as a member of his crew.

It all seemed fantastic now. That other Wilson Bersey seemed to be a vision out of a nightmare. The present Wilson Bersey, respected and encouraged by his employers, who expected big things of him, certainly had no kinship with that young snob of a globe-trotter or with that spineless youth who fell so low as to try to become a rum-runner. The present Wilson Bersey, master and chum of Pieface, could not even

think without a shudder of that half-crazed
boy who tried to drown Pieface.

And it was Pieface who had played the
most important part in bringing about this
transformation. It was Pieface who had
showed him the way to live at sea. And
through learning to live at sea he had
learned to live on shore.

He shook his head, wondering at himself
and at life in general, and picked up his
newspaper. Pieface rubbed against his legs,
and he stroked the dog as he read. He
scanned various items of news.

Suddenly his hand stopped in its patting
of Pieface's head, and he sat up with a
start.

"Pieface," he ejaculated, "will you listen
to this?"

Pieface listened. He always listened
when Wilson talked.

"Rum-runner captured; crew arrested,"
Wilson read the headline.

"The schooner 'Nancy Noel,' Captain
Eric Smith, was captured by coast guardsmen today after a thrilling race just outside
Boston Harbor. A large quantity of liquor
was seized, and eight members of the crew

were arrested, in addition to the captain."
This Wilson read.

"Pieface," he said, "that's what I missed.
That's the same ship that I tried to ship
on at Miquelon. Whew?"

He read on: "The rum-runners submitted peacefully after their schooner had been
overhauled by the coast-guard cutter, with
the exception of one sailor, who attempted
to fight his way to freedom and succeeded
only in being booked on the additional
charge of resisting an officer. He gave his
name as Percy Peters, but was more ap-
propriately called 'Plugugly' by his shipmates."

"Plugugly Peters!" Wilson cried. "That's
what became of him. What do you know
about that, Pieface?"

At the mention of the familiar name of
the former mate, Pieface had displayed
his only interest in the story Wilson was
reading. He growled menacingly at that,
and turned around to make sure that his
old enemy had not entered the room. Finding the room still free from such a presence, he turned back to Wilson.

Wilson was reading on. He read the

names of the other members of the crew,
the amount of liquor seized, the details of
the chase. But Pieface had no further interest. He listened, but he listened impatiently. He wished the reading would end.

Finally he tugged lightly at Wilson's
trouser leg.

"All right, old boy, we'll go," said Wilson.

He knew that Pieface was eager to be
off for their daily walk to the waterfront
where he could fill his lungs with the sweet
sea air, and where he could gaze out into
the harbor into which would one day sail
the captain's ship—his ship.

This was Pieface's greatest pleasure of
the day—every day. He was still the sea
dog.

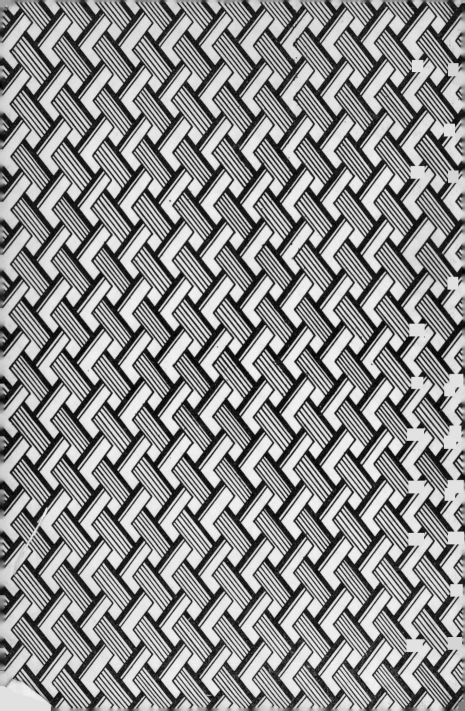